By the same Author (in French)

Théâtre
L'annonce faite à Mukoko *ou Mbulu-Mbulu* & Quand le bras est malade, Paris, BoD, 2019.
Matricule 22, Paris, BoD, 2018.
Les Trois francs *ou Malanda de Mbenseke,* Paris, BoD, 2018.
Les Princes de Mbanza-Kongo, Paris, BoD, 2018.
Liberté, *procès intemporel contre l'asservissement de l'homme (noir),* Paris, BoD, 2018.
Tchimpa-Vita ou *les préparatifs du bûcher de Kilombo, Paris, BoD, 2018.*
Théâtre - Oeuvre complète, Paris BoD, 2020.

Roman
Le Troisième Jour, *Plaidoirie pro domo, Paris,* BoD, 2018.

Récit
L'exode, *Bisi Mavula,* Paris, BoD, 2019.

Proverbes
Le Masque des mots *sous le toit de mon père* (traduction de proverbes Kongo), Paris, BoD, 2018.

Histoire
Brazzaville *Cœur de la nation congolaise* 1880-1970, Paris, BoD, 2018.

Essai
Georges Brassens, *les diables s'en mêlent à présent,* Paris, BoD, 2018.

Poésie
Du pays d'où nous venons, *poésie à deux mains* (avec Benoist S. Lhoni), Paris, BoD, 2018.

Contes
Guirlandes fanées (*Contes du Congo-Brazzaville*), Acoria, Paris, 2011.
Guirlandes fanées (*Contes & légendes du Congo-Brazzaville*), Nlle édition, BoD, Paris 2018.
Tales and Legends Kôngo (Congo-Brazzaville), BoD, Paris, 2021.

Tales & Legends Kôngo

(Congo-Brazzaville)

Born in Congo-Brazzaville (1929-1976). Between 1950 and 1960, he took part in Congolese literary movements, notably in *Liaison* (magazine of AEF cultural circles) which he directed in its last year. He co-founded the *Institute of Congolese Studies* (1960) and the *Congolese Theatre Centre* (1964). He was responsible for the cultural service of Brazzaville City until 1976.

Translated from Kôngo and French
by ***Benoist Saul Lhoni***
original title : **Guirlandes Fanées**
(Contes et légendes du Congo-Brazzaville)

Cover image : © Ray-M' — **Cover :** © Allan Geordy.
Illustration: St Léo / Ray-M' / Geordy

Book produced by ACGI graphic workshops
On behalf of and under Benoist Saul Lhoni direction.

Edition : Books on Demand
12/14 Rond-point des Champs-Élysées, 75008 Paris
Printed by BoD (Books on Demand)
Norderstedt, Deutschland
ISBN: **978-2-3224-098-22**
Legal deposit: February 2022

Tales and Legends Kôngo

(Congo Brazzaville)

Patrice Joseph Lhoni

Mbônghi

2
Tome

Ray-Mi

The people who made them have long since moved on to other lands. And they have faded in the sun, due to lack of maintenance.

Patrice Lhoni

Vestiges of a cultural splendour three quarters already buried in the past, because according to Amadou Hampâté Ba: '*In Africa, an old man who dies is a library that burns*' (UNESCO Tribune, 1960).

Ray-M'

The letter below led the author to collect the tales he was thinking of calling: The Book of the Little Ones.

Brazzaville, 12 March 1974

Sister,

Mail for mail, I answer you through Sixtine (Siki) hand who has the advantage over me, of being able to write. Thank you for the postcard to the little inhabitants of Touraine!

Dame! What dizzy Edgard (Eddy) is! I'll tell you why: When the mailman arrived at our house, I was at the neighbours' house at my age (you can guess, what for). Eddy ran to tell me that I had a toy from France, i.e. from you! Poor Eddy! He still doesn't know the difference between a postcard and a toy! You see my disappointment…

So, it's with tears that I answer you

Signed: Constant-Francis-Jacob Lhoni.

To my children

How happy I will be
To my grave,
If they remember,
Everywhere and always,
That they're from here,
And not from elsewhere!
Paternal heritage
Very derisory!
However, I attach to it
More value to it
Than all the golds of the world:
It's a viaticum of life

Foreword

I was a candidate (an unfortunate one) in a preselection competition for the *O.R.T.F.* (Office de Radiodiffusion-Télévision Française). The jury asked me this question (I think I can quote it verbatim): '*Do you think that the* Fables de La Fontaine *would appeal, to little Africans?*' I replied almost without missing a beat: But why not? And for at least three reasons: everything that is a tale, legend or fable flatters the imagination of the child generally; La Fontaine makes animals speak in most of his fables, and in most African tales animals are the main heroes...

I would like to make a small personal remark: it's wrong to believe that La Fontaine wrote his fables only for children...

Indeed, tales reflect the soul of a people. They're the expression of its mythologies, its gods, its taboos, suggested as models to follow in society. The tales present us with a marvellous universe where beasts and things, spirit and inert matter acts and triumphs: none obstacles are insurmountable; no problems are unsolvable; life unfolds in defiance of all adversity. We are, through the tales, introduced to a perfect world. To tell the truth, cunning, wickedness, injustice, and all human defects given free rein, so that we learn to hate them. Thus, with the tales, we're in the school of the Wise...

Our ancestors would have been mistaken for having more heart than head. They had, rather, as many heads as hearts. They also, had as many ears as mouths. They talked and talked endlessly: for pleasure as much as for the enrichment of their fine, tirelessly strained ears. But their chatter was always useful to teach their children to integrate into society; to denounce human vices; they spoke to them an absurd language, contrary to common sense, because they gave a speech to voiceless beings and made inanimate things perform great acts. Deliberately refusing to play the game of abstractions, they willingly resorted to the figurative style... Societies with a strong imagination invented tales (but what people, moreover, don't have their tales?) That is to say fantastic stories. In which the actions take place and the characters evolve in an unreal world. Often, these characters aren't so much human persons as animals or birds gifted with speech and reason.

But when it comes to fairy tales, we shouldn't be mistaken: devious minds skilfully exploit what passes for popular wisdom, with the sole sordid aim of maintaining or safeguarding their already advantageous social status. The tale then becomes their slavish instrument, to lull the naive to sleep! For, in truth, the strength of Lûbu beating Nzâu in battle is nothing just a falsehood! When Mfûlu challenges Nkâbi to match him in the sprint, did she make a bad joke?

Never, under other skies or in living memory, have shepherdesses married charming princes! The fundamental question is, therefore, who uses the tale and in whose favour it's pictured? The tale, precisely, only truly fulfils its social vocation insofar as it truly and fully expresses a popular feeling, and helps to respond to it...

However, one would like to think that storytelling was only specific to pastoral societies. In other words, the tale would only flourish at the origin of humanity, within the so-called primitive human cells.

It also means that the story would play an increasingly limited role as people progress in their technical and scientific development. Such reasoning is absurd, because even in its naive form, the tale is educational. That is its primary function. And what community, whether primitive, antique, modern or industrialised, doesn't have a desire for moral health?

What are the theatre, the cinema, the carnival and other types of entertainment, if not so many events designed to restore the image of the feelings nobility? And, at the same time, to respond to the need for the so-called developed societies escape; they have to deal with their daily truths and vicissitudes. If these performances tend to exaggerate or distort reality, how do they diverge from the spirit from which the tale proceeds?

All the great classical playwrights took their inspiration from the mythologies of their respective environments...

Thus, the tale, like the classical theatre, deals with the universal feelings of the humanity: love, emotion, passion, bravery and all the vices and virtues. Classical theatre, like the fairy tale, exalts virtue and ridicules shortcomings. Both aim at the same goal: to instruct and perfect the young candidates for life. To put the misguided spirits back on the right track.

However, to remain educational, the tale must remain, above all, attractive, like all teaching. A good tale combines the useful with the pleasant. It must therefore entertain as well as instruct.

To entertain : This is why: not everyone can tell. The storyteller is an actor, that is to say: an interpreter. But instead of presenting the characters involved, he has to embody them. His role appears to be twofold: he does not only act, he must live the action. His mission is only fully assumed under this double condition. He ceases to be a discreet translator: he's directly concerned; he must therefore commit himself. He's all at the same time: interpreter, author or creator or inventor, animator and responsible...

Of the storyteller, the qualities of the modern comedian: intelligence and sensitivity required for the interest or the effectiveness of his role. What am I saying? It was the primitive or pastoral storyteller who gave birth to the contemporary actor. The latter has only the advantage of the scientific, technical and material means development at his disposal; and of the abundance or his repertoire diversity, which enriched over the ages; through contact with various civilisations.

But some tales are true human dramas. How, then, can they render effectively if the storyteller is devoid of intelligence and sensitivity? He must therefore know how to tell the facts; know how to colour them; know how to dress them up according to the circumstances of the time and place and, seizing every favourable opportunity, resort, if necessary, to the pictorial expression... It's therefore not enough to speak in a monotone. For speaking alone isn't enough.

The use of songs seems to be salutary in such cases. It's associated with the success of the cause. It's therefore necessary to sing. From then on, the storyteller sometimes speaks, sometimes sings. But the true storyteller doesn't intend to play alone. He invites his audience to participate in the action. He then sets himself up as a soloist, facing the chorus of spectators. The chorus alternates with the responses. This creates a lively atmosphere of joyfulness and intense communion. Soon there are no longer any actors on one side or assistants on the other. The goal reached and shared by all.

But this would still not be enough if the actor failed to add a demonstration to his words or songs. And the storyteller runs, jumps, if he has to run or jump; he laughs or cries, if he has to laugh or cry, and... dies, if he has to die! This isn't yet enough. For in order to be better at his job (it's a job), the storyteller sometimes imitates the feline walk of the lion, the panther or the Ngô, occasionally the barking of the Mbuâ, or the meowing of the cat, or the sad yapping of the jackal, the mournful howling of the owl, etc.

But what else? The storyteller has to become a marauder (alas, yes!) with the Nkêwa, whose guilty gesture he has to imitate unequivocally. He plays the role of the cunning with the Nchiêchié in his skill tricks at the expense of the Ngô. In short, the storyteller must be part of all this and more: wise man, thief, liar, idiot, blackmailers, dancer, orator, justiciar and vigilante...

The audience no longer just follows. It lives with passion all these multiple and varied situations in which the storyteller has led and drawn him thanks to his know-how, his particular gifts. They allow him to exploit and take advantage of the episode or the pathetic drama of his story.

We can see, our traditional conception of drama breaks with the conveniences or classic conventions of modern shows, whose interpretation requires cleverly staged performances beforehand.

So much for the charming side of the tale. But what lies beneath the appeal?

To instruct: The tale is, in its banter form, as I have already said, didactic. But it's a very flexible mode of teaching. If it's open to all, it's indirectly given and therefore optionally received; thus putting masters and disciples off the beaten track of dogmas and doctrines. The old man reviews his conduct, the child learns about life, the innocent finds moral comfort and a source of encouragement to persevere on the right path, while the wrongdoer hears the stern voice of his conscience.

Moreover, the tale is allegorical, in the sense that it doesn't always directly address the truth it intends to reveal. It's therefore in a fictitious universe that the tale takes us, that of animals or birds, although, all in all, they appear familiar to us in certain ways.

The improbable, on the other hand, are the actions skilfully carried out by beings naturally devoid of intelligence, and which, in reality, are moved only by their instinct. But here: Mbôma, Ngômbulu, Ngô, Nzâu, Ngûvu, Nkêwa, Nchiêchié, Nkâbi, Mbûlu, Mbêmba, Kûti, Ntiêtié, Nkôkotuvi, Mfûlu, Nkômbo, Lunguênia, Nsûsu, Mbuâ, Mbûma, etc., act as persons endowed with human reason.

All these beasts lead a human life, have the qualities or the defects of humans. To each animal is assigned the character proper to the social rank it represents:

Ngômbulu is the king. It rages.

Ngô is powerful; It's evil and know only the law of the strongest.

But if Nzâu is majestic, it doesn't foolishly take pride in its mass of flesh; it's intelligence itself, combined with bonhomie.

Nchiêchié is cunning and easily gets out of trouble; it misleads by its devious mind.

Mfûlu hides many tricks under its apparent heaviness.

Nkêwa is mischievous, and smells a trap.

Nkâbi is stupid; it's the innocent victim of the great ones malice when it isn't the victim of the small ones cunning.

Mbôma, and Ngûvu are naive, even if they're presumptuous.

Tchîula is ingenious...

They're symbols. In truth, through these beasts of creation, human persons parade, with their traits: goodness, badness, honesty, cunning, lies, calumny, backbiting, deceit...

Thus, through the tale, virtue is exalted, while vice is held in abhorrence. Because of this, the tale is moral. Its unfolding, through its twists and turns, leads us to love greatness or nobility of soul, and to despise eccentricity and mediocrity. But to achieve its goal, the tale proceeds by induction: it goes from the particular to the general and, stripping itself of all artifice, extrapolates. In many cases, morality is implied.

But, as I have pointed out, tell alone isn't enough; you have to add the art of eloquence, the oratory talent, to enthral and obsess. Thus the tale is the basis of our anthology. It's the starting point of our literature which, however oral it may be, isn't less, a living expression, that is to say an effective communication means or the truth transmission. It's a whole school. If it doesn't teach science or technique, it forms men in the full word sense, worthy of their society.

Brief animal glossary Kôngo/English

[1] – Dingânsengo, *Mason Wasp*
Kûku-Mpêla, *Cuckoo*
Kitômbo, *Kingfisher*
Kûti, *Owl*
Lûbu, *Mosquito*
Lubûkuyongo, *Whippoorwill*
Lumbuê, *Hawk*
Lumpfîkini, *Bat*
Lunguênia, *Chameleon*
Mbêmba, *Eagle*
Mbôma, *Boa*
Mbuâ, *Dog*
Mbûlu, *Jackal*
Mbûma, *Cat*
Mfuênghe, *Weasel*
Mfûlu, *Turtle*
Mpûku, *Rat*
Munghângha, *Crow*
Nchiêchié, *Gazelle*

Ndingâ, *African Green Pigeon*
Nghêmbo, *Dogfish*
Ngô, *Leopard*
Ngômbulu, *Lion*
Ngôngolo, *Centipede*
Nguâri, *Partridge*
Ngûndum'nua, *Nightingale*
Ngûvu, *Hippopotamus*
Niânzi, *Fly*
Nkâbi, *Antelope*
Nkêlele, *Guinea fowl*
Nkêwa, *Monkey*
Nkôkotuvi, *Dud beetle*
Nkômbo, *Billy Goat*
Nkônko, *Grasshopper, Locust*
Nkûmbi, *Garden dormouse, Lerot*
Nsuêle, *Quail*
Nsûsu, *Rooster*
Ntchîbizi, *Hedgehog, Grass cutter*
Ntiêtié, *Wren*
Nûni, *bird, birds*
Nzâu, *Elephant*
Pôpori, *Warbler garden*
Tchigâla, Lizard
Tchidûkia, *Dove*
Tchimbêmbe, *Falcon*
Tchindôngo (sing), Bindôngo (pl.), *Sheep*
Tchingôngo, *Woodpecker*

Contents

Tales

Legends

Tales

I have translated the following tales, without any pretence or literary elegance: they have enough moral vigour in themselves.

Nchiêchié
Nkûmbi na Ngô

They lived in the same village.

One day, Ngô invited Nchiêchié to go and work in the field. It refused. Ngô took a hoe, a cutter and an axe. It worked alone in the field. It cut down the trees, cut the vines, mowed the grass, and set fire to the brush. Once this first task accomplished, Ngô planted fruit trees which soon grew and produced fruit.

Nchiêchié, who was walking through the forest, came across Ngô plantation. The trees were full of beautiful ripe fruit. Nchiêchié couldn't resist the temptation to eat them. It went up to the trees and picked a good harvest. Afterwards, it set off on its merry way. Which led it to the foot of a palm tree where it met Nkûmbi:

— Here! Eat them, you'll tell me if they're bad!

As it said this, Nchiêchié slipped some fruit into Nkûmbi paws.

— Hm! How delicious they are! Nkûmbi said loudly, having just bitten into them. *But tell me where you picked them.*

— In Uncle Ngô plantation! And if you want to see it, oh, it's a beautiful plantation! Come with me! It's not far from here. You'll agree with me that it's beautiful work. Come on!

In a few trots, they arrive at the foot of the trees. Whose branches are bending under the weight of the fruit. Under the sting of the demon temptation, Nchiêchié and Nkûmbi climb the trees and strip them. But in its feverish haste, Nkûmbi let a fruit fall to the ground. Ngô is nearby and attracted by the noise. In a few jumps, it's in its plantation:

— Who is up there?

— It's me, Nchiêchié!

— And what are you doing up there?

— I... I...

— *Yes, yes! But didn't I ask you to come and work with me? Only you refused, because you're lazy and you're afraid to work under the sun! But now the fruit is good, isn't it?*

— *Yes, Uncle. But that's an understatement: they're tempting!*

— *Yes, yes, but wait for me up there!*

But, glancing around at the other trees, Ngô also saw Nkûmbi:

— *Ah, well, you too?*

— *Yes, Uncle, on the advice and guidance of Nchiêchié!*

— *Come down, both of you!*

Nkûmbi prepares to go down. But when it gets close to the ground, it makes a leap and takes off! Ngô pursues it, but in vain, because Nkûmbi has hastily gone into a burrow, blessing its forebears with the domestic inheritance!

— *Now it's just the two of us,* Ngô shouted at Nchiêchié.

— *I'm coming, but listen to me, and pay close attention! If you hear a heavy noise, it's me. If the noise muffled, then it's only my bag.*

— *Get down! I tell you, and go elsewhere!*

Nchiêchié drops its bag full of fruit. At the

heavy sound of the bag, Ngô shouts, adding its demonstration to its words:

— *Hang the thief!*

But, at the same time, Nchiêchié, who lets itself fall with a loud noise, picks itself up and runs away!

— *Well done!* It said.

Pitying, Ngô is angry and goes back home. But it promises to teach Nchiêchié a lesson. It goes to its house, grabs it, shakes it, manhandles it:

— *You will pay for your mischief with your life!*

And Ngô locks Nchiêchié in a bag, and goes to drown it in the river, in the middle of the river!

On the way, Ngô wanted to smoke its pipe. But it has no fire with it. As it approaches a village, it puts down its burden at the side of the road and runs to light its pipe.

Nzôbo, who was in the vicinity, passed by the place where the bag was lying. The scene it saw amused it greatly, and made it, laugh to tears:

— *Hi! Hi! Hi! We've seen it all with you! What other trick are you up to? Do you have to lock yourself in a bag now? But who are you trying to fool again?*

— *Nobody at all! And my present situation is sadder than you know. Do you think that I'm in this sack for fun? Because, you see, Ngô had the curious idea. Making me, the queen of all the animals in creation! You bet! Me, queen? I'm not well. I'm not better like that, eh, tell me! So I declined Ngô largesse. Dame! The old villain isn't at all happy and, to punish me, well; here I'm in a bag!*

— *You were wrong to disappoint Ngô, for who can refuse honours if, a fortiori, they elevate you to royal dignity?*

— *Whoa! So you would have accepted them!*

— *And how so! And on the spot, and on the hour!*

— *In this case, let's agree! Put me back in this bag and, from here, I'll join my rank!*

Nzôbo likes honours. It stuffs itself into the bag. Without any ulterior motive, to the great relief of Nchiêchié. Who says to it, not without a touch of irony:

— *Farewell, my beautiful queen!*

Nchiêchié returns to its home. But on its return, Ngô wants nothing to do with the change that took place in its absence. Instead, it sneers.

— *Ah! Ah! They would like to fool me again! Time and effort wasted! My decision is categorical, irrevocable: to the river, and in the middle of the river! I have no more use for pranks which have gone on long enough and which, if they have entertained some, must now be sanctioned. One doesn't make fun of Ngô with impunity!*

— Brother Ngô, I'm indeed the unfortunate Nzôbo. Set me free, I beg you! I have been fooled by Nchiêchié tricks! It told me that you punished it by locking it up in this bag, because it refused the honour you gave it, of being all the animals queen on earth. I was tempted by such generosity and…

— Speak! Speak! You have time! And I hear you well, but you will be queen despite yourself, at the bottom of the waves!

With that, Ngô loads its burden on its shoulder. It walks with determination to the edge of the river. On a drifting pirogue, it takes its place, arrives in the middle of the river, and drowns Nchiêchié.

On the way back, Ngô hurriedly went to make an inventory of Nchiêchié belongings, and to appropriate them. But it was taken, who thought it was taken! Ngô can't believe its eyes when Nchiêchié, visibly delighted, comes to meet it:

— Ah, my dear uncle Ngô, why didn't you throw

me much further out into the river, whose bed conceals an infinite and indescribable quantity of unsuspected riches! Believe me or not, but the truth is that the mountains of gold, silver, copper, diamonds, and everything else that is precious, make it a wonderful universe. But the genius who watches over this fabulous empire doesn't tolerate staying there for more than half a day. That is why I returned so quickly. I had barely enough time to take these few drapes and blankets with golden fringes. But suddenly I'm richer than before! And that is thanks to you, my dearest and most esteemed uncle! But can I thank you?

Ngô is pensive. But if it's offended, it's also tempted to get rich like Nchiêchié:

— *It's incredible, even unheard of! You won't say that heaven has provided you badly! And when, having wanted to send you to your death, I have served to increase your fortune, to transform your last days into happy days, I'm tempted to cut short my life! But what reward do you promise me in return, since you now owe me a flourishing life?*

— *Well, anything you like, anything! Only speak.*

— *You couldn't refuse, for example, to go... uh... throw me in the middle of the same river, could you?*

— The new situation I owe you forbid me to displease you. That's the least I can say.

— So, let's make it quick! I'm looking forward to getting rich like you. But I beg you to throw me in the real middle of the river, will you?

— The pleasure is all mine, and I will know how to fulfil your wishes!

But Ngô sank in the water like a large stone. Nchiêchié inherited all its possessions, including its spouses!

This story is sad, because it punishes the one who was in its most legitimate right. However, neither strength nor cunning can take precedence over law.

Tchîula Na Mbôma

As hunger nagged at it, Mbôma went hunting. Unwinding its long ribbon of gold and ash grey, it set off towards the game bushes. But it had to wander for a long time in the thickets, as the game was scarce. Tiredness added to hunger, it

felt the need to take some rest at the foot of a tree. But no sooner did it lie down there than the tree collapsed and beat down on it with all its weight. All its efforts to free itself were in vain, and it was forced to remain under the stunner.

Nsîbizi, who was frolicking and frolicking in the vicinity, ventured near the suffering Mbôma:

— *Isn't Master Mbôma that my eyes see?*

— *It's me!*

— *And what are you doing under the tree?*

— *Well, I wanted to rest at the foot of this tree when suddenly it fell on me! You speak of a misfortune that never comes alone! For I'm hungry and on the hunt. But that's it!*

— Would you like me to get you out of here?

— Useless question, and as soon as possible!

— Yes, but I'm afraid you'll throw yourself at me once you're free!

— That's the way to thank your benefactors! Master Mbôma was indignant.

But, cautious, Nsîbizi moved, leaving Mbôma under its tree. It remembered many nasty trick of the monster whose reputation is to suffocate its innocent victims under its powerful embrace!

Skipping here and there, Tchîula arrives at the tree, lying down in its entirety:

— My word! Unless my eyes deceive me, it's indeed Lord Mbôma that I see! And what is it doing under the tree? Hello, Lord of the Mbôma!

— Alas! Yes, the unfortunate Lord of the Mbôma that I'm now!

— But what on earth has happened to you?

— I'm asking myself that too!

— Do you need any help?

— But do I have to say it, in such a situation? Is my situation not alarming enough? Then, isn't

helping all the more pleasant, all the more appreciable and precious, the more prompt and spontaneous it is?

— Of course it is. But generosity is poorly paid for in return! So isn't my right to take precautions and to suspect the intentions of others? For, perhaps you should be reminded, your name is Mbôma, isn't it?

— So what?

— So, you aren't new, under the sun. And you aren't known to our world…

— Ah, please, and enough of this philosophy! And what does it matter in front of a soul in pain, even if it's from Mbôma? Is it in my nature to be ungrateful? Come on, then! You don't hurt whoever helps you, come on!

Mbôma gentle language convinced Tchîula, who felt it had a soul. It will take its saving action. It goes under the tree, and gradually lifts it with all the strength of its arched back and its stiffened legs. Mbôma frees itself, as Tchîula succeeds in its efforts. But, when it's saved, the monster falls on its benefactor!

— For a comedy, it's good! So, to thank me, you see fit to eat me! What conscience is yours?

— Reason, my friend, reason! One isn't so

foolish and naive as to philosophise about kindness, generosity and gratitude! Hunger is the cause of my misadventure. But who said that a hungry stomach has no ears? Ah, the beautiful maxim! And for two days I have put nothing in my stomach; nothing at all, my friend. Nothing! So you speak of the good fortune you represent for me! The pleasure of moralising is yours!

With this speech, Master Mbôma began to eat Tchîula, first taking care to wet it with its saliva, to swallow it more easily. But just as it was about to swallow its prey, the latter still had the time and courage to speak to it:

— *You probably think you're very clever by abusing my kindness. I would like, despite everything, to do you one last favour. Listen: From now on, avoid standing under crumbling trees, otherwise...*

Meanwhile, and before Tchîula had finished its exhortation, Nchiêchié arrived:

— *Would it be an indiscretion to ask you what you two are doing?* Asks the beautiful curious with the fine muzzle, the mischievous eye, and who is said to drink from its pointed hoof.

Tchîula, who, despite the circumstances, hasn't lost the use of its tongue, replies.

— *The other was dying under the big tree weight that fell on it. I lent it to my good services, and to thank me in its way, it's eating me!*

— *Strange habits, indeed!* Nchiêchié said and added, addressing Tchîula:

— *But you're not going to make me believe that you could lift a tree of that size!*

— *Yes, I could! Yes, I could! Besides, Mbôma itself can testify, if it wants to answer you!*

— *No! I don't need it to talk to me! The best proof of your strength feat, you alone can give it, by doing the number again, so that I can see with my eyes how you managed to lift this giant!*

— *But I'm ready and willing to demonstrate!*

— *Yes, but not without Mbôma under the tree!*

And while the scene was being reconstructed, Nchiêchié ordered the batrachian to drop the heavy stunner trap! Tchîula complied without being told twice and, *bvûba*! The tree crushed Mbôma!

— *Farewell, ingrate! Tchîula croaks again. I must be stupid and naive twice for you to take me back!*

Mbuâ
M'Tînu Bibûlu

Once, Mbuâ was king. One day, all the animals had gathered in the court of the monarch, who had summoned them to review with them the general progress of the kingdom's affairs.

Mfûlu, whose absence noted during the great assembly, didn't arrive until it was about to end. But this voluntary lateness of Mfûlu was a calculation intended to provoke the unpopularity and, consequently, the fall of the king whose thousand and one defects it knew and hated. For, according to its wish, someone other than Mbuâ would have been more deserving of being chosen to carry the sceptre, in the name of the animals. So, in its premeditated intention to entice Mbuâ, for ridiculing it, Mfûlu had taken the precaution of carrying a bone in its bag.

The king, for its part, considered the lateness to be an obvious challenge, reflecting a notorious act of insubordination, which it wanted to sanction in an exemplary manner. But Mfûlu hadn't yet arrived at court when it threw the bone to Its Royal Majesty, while apologising for the lateness and begging the king's indulgence. Putting its words into action, it said:

— *Here, Sire, is the object of my lateness. At the end of a successful fight in which I took an active part, it's the whole share of the booty that has been allocated to me! My protest gave rise to an interminable palaver, the cause of my lateness...*

The sight of the bone made Mbuâ greedy fangs snap. It forgot its dignity and left the throne from which it was presiding over the meeting. It leapt at the bait, and went off to crush it with a clatter of jaws. Punctuated by grunts of pleasure. To the great scandal of all the subjects!

— *And it's our king!* They're indignant, a king without scruples! *It's so greedy that, in the face of so little, it can no longer contain itself and allows itself to be dishonoured! A bone, because of a bone, nothing more, and it has forgotten itself!*

But the mockery and derogatory reflections of its subjects make the king angry. As a result, it orders its close associates to punish, severely, all animals whose behaviour constitutes a capital offence!

Aware of its guilt and the seriousness situation, Mfûlu fled and ran to hide in its house.

Ngômbé took an axe and cut off Sloth's tail. It also attacked Niôka, cut off its limbs, then stretched it: Niôka became a long crawling ribbon.

Mbôma bludgeoned Ngûlu M'Chîtu head, whose snout grew longer. It also seized Mbêmba and threw it into the air. Finally, Mbôma flanked Yânga against a stone where it was flattened.

M'Nûnzi, in turn, had to deal with Nchiêchié, who plunged it into a pot containing stinking resin, after having pulled its nose, which lengthened.

Tchîula tried to flee, but it was intercepted by Mpâkassa who led it before the king. It was made to sit down on the ground so roughly that its limbs were twisted to the point that it could no longer stand up.

Nkêwa found refuge in the dense foliage of a tree. Where it remained until the end of the reprisals...

Since that time, all animals, large and small, bear the scars of the violence of which they were victims, and which now characterise them:

The Sloth has no tail.

Niôka is limbless.

Ngûlu M'Chîtu has only a piece of amputated snout.

Mbêmba always flies. If it lands somewhere, its legs tremble.

Yânga is flat.

M'Nunzi smells bad. If it has an elongated nose, it's because it was pulled by the mouth of the resin pot in which it was immersed.

Tchîula drags itself like a baby, because its limbs were twisted.

Nkêwa jumps from branch to branch.

Ngô
Na Nchiêchié

— *Let's set up a business that pays!* Suggested Ngô.

— *What business, for example?* Nchiêchié asked

— *We could buy and raise goats and billy goats.*

— *So let's buy and raise goats and billy goats!*

— *Yes, but be careful!*

— *Why?*

— *Well, you will only have to buy goats, while I will only buy billy goats.* But we will raise them and graze them together.

Nchiêchié agreed to the concession. It bought the goats. Ngô bought the billy goats.

The animals were parked together.

Nchiêchié goats multiplied, while Ngô goats decreased in number and, by eating them one by one, the shepherd ended up exterminating its herd!

Deprived, Ngô attacked Nchiêchié goats. But, as with its billy goats, each time it slaughtered them, it feasted on itself. Ngô is selfish.

But, tired, eventually, of always having to get up at night to go and steal Nchiêchié goats, Ngô thought it had found a way of sparing itself its nocturnal exercises. By inviting its girlfriend to take the state of the herds stock:

— *Let's count our animals and proceed with the sharing*, said Ngô, but in a threatening tone, bordering on a declaration of war.

Nchiêchié was startled:

— *What animals?*

— *Haven't they multiplied and intermingled with each other? It's therefore good that each takes its own and parks them separately!*

— *But only my goats have multiplied! As for your billy goats, not only have you eaten them all...*

— *Shut up! This isn't the time for speeches. But let them hear us instead!*

Ngô goes off to find judges. Nzâu, Nkâbi and Nzôbo, all friends of Ngô, soon arrive in the village.

— *I have an argument with Nchiêchié. I ask you to settle it for us.*

— *Wait until I too go and call my people,* said Nchiêchié, who leaves immediately.

At the exit of the village, it meets Lumpfîkini.

— *Where are you running to, in such a hurry?*

— *Let me first explain what is happening to me: Ngô and I live in the same village. We raise animals there and they live together. That's fine. But, an important detail, we agreed that Ngô (on its proposal) would only raise billy goats, and I would only raise goats. Right. But not only did Ngô exterminate its herd, eating one animal after the other, it also started to clear out mine. And now — and this is the crux of my concern — Ngô is inviting me to count the animals and to divide them up!*

I don't want to know anything, since only my goats have reproduced. Ngô supports the absurd. Because according to it, its goats have also given birth! It sent for its friends Nzâu, Nkâbi and Nzôbo, to get us to agree. And so, I run to look for my friends, so that they can assist me before the court of justice convened by Ngô.

— *Go back to your village,* said Lumpfîkini. *I will meet you there in a moment.*

Seeing Nchiêchié return, Ngô exclaimed:

— *Nchiêchié entered Lumpfîkini house, but it ran out!*

At the same time, Lumpfîkini passes by. Nzâu says to it:

— *Why don't you stop although you see people gathered?*

— *You're right,* agrees Lumpfîkini. *But I'm in a hurry. I'm running to call my mother, because my father, whose pregnancy is at full term, is due to give birth at any moment!*

Nzâu shouts in astonishment:

— *What? ? ? How can you make such nonsense? Repeat what you have just said, so that my friends here can hear it!*

— *Yes! I say will call my mother because my father is about to give birth!*

— *Oho!* Exclaimed Ngô judges. *Has anyone seen a male giving birth since the world began? That would be extraordinary!*

— *Yes! As extraordinary as Ngô billy goats giving birth! To the best of your hearing, goodbye!*

Mbêmba And Kûti

In time immemorial when they could speak, all the birds lived together on the same tree. Mbêmba was their king. In the hierarchy of the kingdom, Kûti enjoyed the honours of the second rank, or, if you like, he was the viceroy.

One day, Mbêmba planned to undertake a journey. But before leaving, he sent for Kûti and said to her:

— *I will go travelling I leave you in charge of the kingdom. If, in my absence, something untoward happens, try to call me back urgently.*

Kûti took note of the royal order, and Mbêmba left. But no sooner had he turned his back than the woodcutters, who had long had the malicious intention of felling the great tree, took counsel:

— *Let's cut it down now that the king has gone! No more opposition to the realisation of our old project!*

The lumberjacks carried out their decision. Armed with axes, they cut the trunk of the tree. Seeing this, Kûti, with a loud cry, called Mbêmba:

— *Come back, O king, come back quickly! Your kingdom is under attack!*

The woodcutters competed with their axes. They were very active. Soon the tree bent over, ready to fall. Kûti, panic-stricken, flew from branch to branch, while the chicks, frightened, shouted in chorus.

Amid the general confusion, the woodcutters worked hard at their task. Kûti redoubled and repeated her calls:

— *O betrayed Majesty, come back quickly, and rather, now than later! The invaders have started a work of the kingdom destruction. Come back! Come back quickly, quickly!*

This time the king heard the call which hurries back to the palace. When he arrives, the tree is about to collapse!

Without waiting, Mbêmba plucks a feather and rubs it on the walls of the tree trunk. A miracle! The tree righted itself on the spot! But it was only just. The king had just saved his kingdom from imminent disaster...

Stunned by the magic trick, the woodcutters fled. Time passed. The king, who feared other misfortunes, no longer dared to leave the kingdom. But he languished with boredom, being prey to inactivity. He found the days long, and his existence gloomy. But at last, no sign of a new threat, and the kingdom had long since regained the face of the serene days. So, shaking off his torpor, Mbêmba attempted a second journey. He sent for Kûti, and said to her:

— *I must, despite myself, travel again. As in the past, I entrust you with the care of the kingdom. Be vigilant and, if a misfortune should happen again, advise me immediately.*

Kûti bowed, not without concern, and the king left. But when he left, the woodcutters were at the foot of the tree. At the first blow of the axe, Kûti began to hoot, inviting the king to return as quickly as possible to his steps:

— *Hou hou hou, he said, in his hoarse voice. Come back quickly! Your enemies have returned, but fiercer, more determined and more frantic than the first time! Come back! Come back!*

The chicks cried in panic together. The woodcutters turned a deaf ear to the plaintive cries of the chicks, who incidentally, they didn't care about at all:

— *Cry! Weep! But you're done for! We will find you!*

—*Hoo hoo hoo!* Shouted Kûti, desperately requiring the king. But his cries were lost in echoes in the desert, and didn't reach Mbêmba ears. In desperation, Kûti tried a last effort, by going to perch on the highest branch of the tree. He wanted to shout as well as he could, but the poor steward had no voice! Mbêmba, had ventured too far, even outside the limits of his kingdom, to hear the desperate prayer.

But kings are magicians. Mbêmba felt his blood tingle; his ears buzzed with tinkling. Then he interpreted these various omens: I believe, he said, that I'm the victim of some misfortune, especially since my last night filled with nightmares, among which was a hallucinating dream; all the little birds had fallen from their nests. The woodcutters, my enemies, have probably returned to cut down the domestic tree, and this time they have succeeded in their diabolical enterprise! I will shorten my journey, although I didn't hear Kûti call.

Mbêmba returned to his kingdom. When he entered the town, he could hear the hurried blows of the axe and the woodcutters triumphant cries. The tree was three quarters bent over! The king moaned bitterly:

— *Good God! They destroyed the kingdom!*

When Mbêmba arrived, the entire tree was on the ground, lying on its side. The fall must have been shattering, for all the branches had broken off. The birds, in their terror, flew away, scattering to the four winds, each having taken its direction. Mbêmba saw no one, for Kûti himself, having given in to the general panic, had deserted the place. The king suddenly experienced the painful feeling of solitude.

This is why, since that time, Mbêmba has interspersed his rounds with incessant movements back to his nest, to ensure his safety.

Thus, the saying goes, with our family obligations:

Mbêmba,
After circling, circling,
Comes back to its nest!
It's the keg that always smells of herring.

Tchidûkia Na Ndingâ

One day, Tchidûkia and Ndingâ, in the company of other birds, went hunting.

The beaters entered the thicket and let the

dogs loose. An antelope raised. Tchidûkia aims, shoots and kills it:

— *I got it!* It gloats.

No! It wasn't you; it was me who killed it! Ndingâ claims.

When the beaters arrive with their panting dogs, tongues hanging out, Tchidûkia is beaming with joy:

— *I shot it point-blank!*

— *It's lying!* Ndingâ replies; *it was I who killed it!*

Upset, Tchidûkia is obliged to remain silent. When the booty shared out, it has to settle for a meagre share.

Another time, the birds are still hunting, an

antelope comes along. Tchidûkia points a gun at it, shoots and kills it:

— *I have it again!* It gloats.

— *It's not true! It's my shot again!*

When the beaters come and ask who exactly killed the game, Tchidûkia, always contradicted by Ndingâ, can hardly say a word:

— *It's always me who kills the game!* Ndingâ argues shamelessly.

A third hunt is organised. The beaters raise a hedgehog who takes the key to the field. Tchidûkia stuns it at point-blank range:

— *I hit it in the heart!*

— *It isn't you, it's me!*

This time again, Tchidûkia must give in. But Ndingâ false pretensions had gone too far. So Tchidûkia resolved, next time, not to fire a shot and to let the game pass.

— *How could she do that? It's my shot that always carries. But the other stolen my honour and my right brazenly all the time ! It's my shot that always carries. Ndingâ, from now on it's your turn to kill the game!*

Tchidûkia stood by her decision. It let a large animal escape, against which the dogs were relentless. But when one of the beaters passed by, Tchidûkia pointed at it:

— *They won't always say that I'm clumsy! Catch this one, for the honour and happiness of my gossip!*

Bang!

The shot went off and struck the beater dead. Ndingâ runs up, hurries, leaps, claiming the right and the honour of having had the merit of shooting the game:

— *It's me again, it's always me who kills my animals!*

Tchidûkia is silent, while Ndingâ exults. At the same time, the beaters appear. But at the sight of the inert man, huddled over itself, its chest ravaged by the rifle, Ndingâ shrinks back:

— *This time, it wasn't me who killed it! It was Tchidûkia's shot!*

Tchidûkia is indignant:

— Oh! But it's always your blow that carries! How is it that this time it wasn't you who killed the game?

Tchidûkia says to the beaters:

— *It's definitely a Ndingâ shot. You heard her speaking earlier, and caught her congratulating herself on her skill!*

Ndingâ questioned Heaven, questioned Earth. She had sentenced herself in advance. She went into debt to pay the price of the dead man!

Any ill-founded claim is like a double-edged knife!

Mfûlu Na Ngûlu

Mfûlu and Ngûlu were two great friends. One day, Mfûlu said to Ngûlu:

— *Can you lend me a certain amount of money that I will return to you in six moons?*

Ngûlu answered it:

— *Of course! Shouldn't friends help each other?* And it untied its purse.

The six moons passed without Mfûlu having honoured its promise: the debt, which was beginning to date, remained unpaid. Tired of waiting, Ngûlu decided to go and find Mfûlu. When Mfûlu heard the news, it said to, its wife:

— When you see Ngûlu coming, collect some cassava leaves to cover me, and appear to be pounding them. But above all be careful not answer, to its questions: make yourself deaf and mute. Then it will get angry, then it will throw everything around it into the bush. And you will cry out in indignation, saying: ah! Ngûlu has thrown away the precious stone that the ancestors left us as an inheritance!

Everything happened as Mfûlu had foreseen: when Ngûlu arrived, she returned to its shell and took the form of a vulgar stone. The woman began to pound cassava leaves on its husband's back.

— *Where is your husband?* Asked Ngûlu.

The woman said nothing.

— *Where is your husband?*

Still no answer.

So Ngûlu got angry and threw everything it could get its hands on into the bush. Mfûlu wife, breaking its silence, starts shouting and crying:

— *Ah! Ngûlu has thrown away the precious stone that the ancestors left us as an inheritance!*

At that very moment, Mfûlu comes out from behind its hut and declares:

— *I would pay you today... but now I have to wait for you to find the precious stone that you have just thrown away in the bush!*

And Ngûlu starts to search everywhere...

That's why all the Ngûlu in the world are always stirring the earth with their snouts, in the hope of finding the famous and alleged precious stone!

Bakâla Na M'Kênto

A man swore on the faith of his wife.

One day, the village chief gathered the people. He asked them:

— *Who among you can tell me if his wife loves him?*

The question embarrassed the villagers, and against all expectations, the chief noticed an embarrassed silence.

— You're all very talkative! But I understand you well.

He was about to send them home when a young man raised his hand and said:

— *I can safely say that my wife loves me.*

I have proof: she does everything I tell her to do; she listens to me; then she's this, and she's that...

— *Good!* Punctuated the chief. *I'm glad to*

hear that at least someone is loved by his wife! Now you can go home.

The next day, the village chief met the young woman whose husband had boasted the day before. He said to her:

— *If I give you earrings, will you accept them?*

— *You can give them to me.*

— *But if your husband sees them, what will you say?*

— *Don't worry! I won't show them to him.*

On the second day, the chief saw the young woman again.

— *If I give you the bracelets, will you accept them?*

— *Yes, I will.*

— *But the day your husband sees them, what will you do?*

— *I will say that it's a gift from my sister.*

On the third day, the young woman and the village chief met again. On this day, in his best and looked younger. As always, the dialogue began.

— *If I asked you to marry me, would you accept?*

The young woman remained pensive. She thought:

— *For three days this man has been giving me presents, and expensive ones at that! Would he spend so much money if he didn't love me? I also know that he's wealthy and, moreover, he's a chef. How many loincloths has my husband bought me since I started living under his roof? If I had been in this man's wife, I would be fulfilled, well dressed and beautifully adorned! So, if I divorce my husband, will I be sold, or cut into pieces?*

After these reflections, she decides:

— *Yes, you could make me your wife.*

But the chief set a condition:

— *You must bring me your husband's head in a m'tete*[1].

— *I will bring it to you.*

The next day, the village chief gathered his subjects again to send them to harvest in his rice field. That day he bought a lot of wine. The villagers drank it until they were thirsty. In the evening, when they returned home, they were all staggering drunk of alcohol. They had never been so drunk.

The young woman had sharpened a knife which, thanks to her husband's drunkenness, she used to decapitate him. She loaded the head into a sheep's head and covered it with a mat. She then went to the village chief to fulfil her condition.

[1] —M'tete = Oblong basket carried by women on their heads.

— You will spend the night in that hut over there, at the back of the courtyard. I'll talk to you in the morning when you wake up.

She spent a restless night: the voice of remorse kept her awake until morning. It isn't so long ago, she thought, that the poor man married me, and I have just given it to death! What will his family say when they hear of his sad fate? Who will pay the dowry? Where will I find the man who will replace him in his family? By asking for a simple divorce, I would have been easily forgivable; I preferred to kill the poor man! Who can prove me, right? If only...

The rooster crowed. It was dawn. The village chief rang the alarm. The villagers gathered in his yard. He had the house where the young woman had spent the night opened. She came out with her head. The village chief called the roll of the villagers. They all of, only one was missing. The chief asked:

— Where is Massîka?

The villagers looked at each other. But he told them:

— Since his wife is here, why don't you ask her what happened to her husband?

The only answer is that she's looking at the mustard covered with a mat. The mustard uncovered. Astonishment!

In the face of general consternation, the chief says:

— *The other day I asked you if your wives loved you. Massîka alone boasted of hers, while you were all perplexed. Now see the love of this woman who killed her husband for bracelets and a pair of earrings!*

Mfûlu, Ngô Na Tchibûbu

Mfûlu neighbours were Tchibûbu and Ngô, whom she feared very much, and whom she would have liked to get rid of, but it was dealing with a strong part. She couldn't think of using force. She therefore resorted to cunning. Here is the stratagem she used to get rid of her terrible neighbours. Meeting Ngô one morning, it said to it:

— *I have to sell you a superior slave. Will you buy it?*

— *I would like to,* Ngô replied. *But first I want to see it.*

— That is impossible today, because it's working on my plantation, half a day away, but tomorrow, at 10 o'clock, find yourself at such and such a place and I will bring it. The one you see with me will be the slave I sell to you. You will only have to take it, but first give me advances according to the custom.

Ngô, who needed a good slave, seduced by Mfûlu fine words. It gave it some textile as a down payment on the price of the sale.

Immediately, Mfûlu ran to Tchibûbu and made it the same proposal as to Ngô.

Tchibûbu accepted. Mfûlu would come to pick him up the next morning to deliver the slave she had just sold him. She left, rubbing her hands together and saying to herself: we will have a good laugh.

The next day, Mfûlu and Tchibûbu were going up and down towards the place where Ngô was waiting for them. And when it saw them coming, it said to itself: Here is by my faith, a gorgeous slave and Mfûlu hadn't lied.

At the same time, it said to Tchibûbu: your slave is over there, you only have to take it away. Ngô and Tchibûbu, both satisfied with their deal, rushed at each other to take possession of their merchandise. They believed that its slave had rebelled, and a terrible struggle ensued in which they both lost their lives. Simultaneously, Mfûlu hurried back to its hut, taking its cloth with it, and rid of its dangerous neighbours.

Kûtu Na Lubû

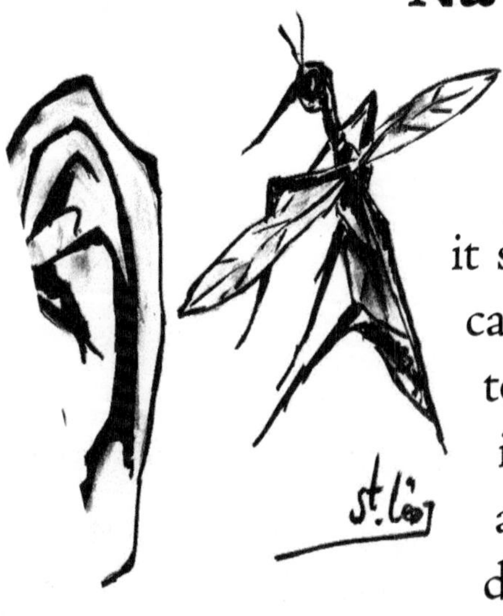

One day, Kûtu gave Lubû some money to help it set up a business. Nkônko came to Lubû, and asked it to lend it this money which it would return to it, it said, as soon as possible. But it didn't keep its promises and, each time Lubû claimed the old debt, Nkônko hastened to reassure it. Always, arguing of its good faith to honour its promise. However, it did nothing.

It is, since that time that Lubû sings its disappointment to Kûtu: it will only pay me tomorrow! it will only pay me tomorrow!

Kûti Na Kitômbo

Kûti made a bet with Kitômbo: if we remain a few days without eating, which of us, do you think, will die first?

Kitômbo replied: Let us put ourselves to the test; let us fast!

But for this purpose, let us go to the bank of a river.

Over the river was a vine, and the two gamblers perched on it.

A fish wriggled on the

surface of the water. Kitômbo flew low into the water and gobbled up the fish. Kûti asked it:

— *What are you doing here?*

— *I lost my balance and to avoid falling, I flew away.*

Another fish came to the surface of the water. Kitômbo flew up, skimmed the water, and gobbled up the fish.

— *What is it now?* Said Kûti.

— *I would go to fall again, and I flew away.*

Kûti died of hunger!

M'Kênto Na Muâ Nûni

A woman was clearing her groundnut field.

But when she returned home, a tiny bird came into the field and replanted the weeds.

This little bird was called the grass transplanter, and as it replanted the grass, it sang about its name:

Ntwîk'ê! Ntwîka masînda!

Ntwîk'ê! Ntwîkidi mô!

(I replant, I replant the herbs!)

The woman went to tell her husband:

— *A little bird comes after me to replant the herbs that I pull up in my field, and the next day, I find a bush in the places I worked the day before! Come and set a trap for it.*

The husband set a trap, and the little bird was caught.

The man was about to kill it, but it begged him:

— *Let me live, I beg you. I could be of some use to you one day!*

Amazed that a bird could speak the language of humans, the man answered its prayer and let it go. But the woman got angry, left her husband, and went home to her parents, never to return. So the husband bought ten calabashes of palm wine to go and fetch his wife. On the way, he met an imp in the guise of a man. Nkûndubulu was his name. He asked the man:

— *Where are you going with so much wine?*

— *I will my parents-in-law's house; to look for my wife.*

— *Wouldn't you like me to come with you!*

— *Come, if you like.*

— *In that case, let me help you carry your wine; give me a calabash.*

No sooner had he taken a few steps hobbling than Nkûndubulu broke the calabash!

— *It's a little incident due to a false step,* he says simply; *and it happens; give me another calabash.*

Without saying a word, the man gave it to him. But, still hobbling, Nkûndubulu broke the second calabash!

— *Give me a third one anyway.*

— *I'm afraid that at this rate you will break them all. And it would be better for me not to go on! As fate would have it, never two without three!*

— *Don't be afraid, however: I was once and for all, a victim of fate; it no longer bears down on me.*

The man thought: I'm experiencing unusual events these days! Where on earth will they take me? But he gave the third calabash. This time Nkûndubulu managed to carry it to the village.

They welcomed in the sacred honour of tradition. Two chickens were killed for them, but they only ate one, keeping the other for the next day, according to the old ancestral wisdom on domestic economy: he who eats in the morning has stocked up the day before! The wine was drunk. He made people sing and dance. The reconciliation of man and woman took place. Nkûndubulu had to spend the night in the hut where the meals were kept. Wasn't this a submission to the test? He ate all the food there, but they didn't look too closely the next day, and they killed another chicken. Then food loaded in the woman's basket, and the man returned to his village.

The time came when the couple had to part

with Nkûndubulu. He was given a good share of the food, but he protested, loudly demanding a share of the woman!

— As we have shared the food, let us share the woman.

An argument broke out between the man and his strange companion. Meanwhile, a multitude of Nkûndubulu arrived:

— So we don't get, along around the common good!

— No! You see, replied Nkûndubulu. He repeated his claims to anyone who would listen. I'm also entitled to my share of the woman!

And all the Nkûndubulu chorused in his favour:

— Nkûndubulu is right! Nkûndubulu is right!

As they were looking for a knife to divide the woman in two, the little herb-breeding bird appeared. He asked:

— What is the object of this tumultuous gathering?

Nkûndubulu said to him:

— *This woman is the object of our quarrel. I have accompanied this man to his parents-in-law's house and we're bringing back, his wife who had left him for some reason. We have been showered with gifts which we have just shared. But I also claim my share of the wife.*

Once again, all the Nkûndubulu were unanimous:

— *Nkûndubulu is right! Nkûndubulu is right!*

— *Yes, that's right,* said the little bird; *I have a knife with me, that will help you to share, but first someone should go and fetch water from the river.*

The referee was applauded. They designated one Nkûndubulu to go to the river. The little bird handed him a calabash. But all the water was leaking out of it! The calabash had a hole in its bottom like a Danaids barrel! Nkûndubulu had to stay at the river for a long time:

— *But what happened to him?* Nkûndubulu became impatient.

Another Nkûndubulu was sent to follow him. This one didn't return either. In despair, the two Nkûndubulu began to sing about their misadventure:

Hey yi bûdikidi é yâya / Nkâlu ya yâ Manguânz'é!

(It's broken, my brother / Brother Manguânza's calabash!)

But, while singing their despair, they danced!

Time passed, and impatience grew among those who were waiting for them. So all the Nkûndubulu went to the river and, in turn, they sang and danced!

The little herb transplanting bird said to the couple:

— *And now, quickly! Quickly! Run away while they're singing and dancing!*

He added, to the man who had set a trap for him:

— *Grateful for gratitude, you owe your salvation to the life I owe you!*

Dingânsengo[2]

Mbuâ, Mpêssé, Nsûsu and Mfuênghe had ordered palm wine from Dintûmbu. They had to come back on the same day to have their drink supplied, at one calabash for each of them.

Mbuâ lived with Nsûsu, and Mfuênghe with Mpêssé. This is why,

2 – Dingânsengo, *Mason Wasp*

at the time fixed by Dintûmbu, they arrived two by two at the hut of M'Sônghi.

Mfuênghe, on seeing Nsûsu, said to itself:

— *Here is my favourite food!*

Nsûsu couldn't resist the temptation, and threw itself on Mpêssé.

Then Mfuênghe pounced on Nsûsu, but to avenge its friend, Mbuâ strangled Mfuênghe.

On her way back from the forest where she had gone to collect wine, Dintûmbu seized with horror: corpses were lying in front of her hut. The gravity of the situation made her lose weight immediately.

Since that day, wasps have a thin waist.

M'Kênto, Mbuâ, Nzâu na Tchisînzila

M'Kênto had two children. One was married, the other was single. She gave each of, them the same money amount. The married child having spent all his money, went to ask the mother's kindness for more. But the mother became angry

and went to complain to the chief of her son's profligacy.

On the way, she met Mbuâ who asked her:

— *Where are you going and where is this great anger coming from?*

M'Kênto replied:

— *Men are strange! I will find the chief to complain about my son who has spent all the money I gave him and is still asking me for more!*

— *You've given me the idea of going to the chief, too. Complaining about the men who only give me the bones of the game after the hunt!*

Having said this, Mbuâ followed in M'Kênto's footsteps and they walked together. They met Nzâu:

— *Where are you going, in such company?*

— *To the chief's house,* they replied. And each of them told him the reason for their journey.

— *Ah, but that's clever! I didn't think of that! Please allow me to share your route, to make myself heard on a case that is particularly close to my heart. Because, you see, despite my size, I never give birth to many little Nzâu during each pregnancy! What does that mean?*

All three left. They saw Tchisînzila in the middle of the road:

— *Where are you going, in such company?*

— *To see the chief.*

And each of them told his concern.

— *I'm also going with you, because I'm not at all happy with those who come to bump into me, only to leave me a few drops of their blood!*

They arrived at their destination at nightfall. The chief showed them where each of them was to spend the night, reserving the sitting of his justice court for the following day.

M'Kênto slept alone in a house. Mbuâ had to watch over a bone. Nzâu was sent to a plantation. Tchisînzila kept the road.

During the night, a snake broke into the house where M'Kênto was sleeping. She began to scream, requiring the men to help her, but no one came to kill the snake, because, according to the chief's instructions, she had to fight it alone, since she hated men.

Nzâu devastated the plantation.

Mbuâ ate the bone.

Tchisînzila injured all the passers-by.

The next morning, the chief held court and called the plaintiffs to appear. M'Kênto presented her accusation. The chief concluded against her:

— *Why were you unable to kill the snake that got into the house where you spent the night? Why did you ask for help from the men, when you came to testify against them?*

M'Kênto had to leave the courtyard, driven away by the men.

It was Nzâu turn to say straight away:

— *Let them tell me why I'm so fat! If I only have to give birth to one little Nzâu every time I get pregnant!*

But at that very moment, the farmers of the plantation ravaged by Nzâu came running. The chief refused to accept its request:

— *Did you hear? You're too greedy. The proof is in others, which you devastated in one night! What would it have been like if you had a numbered litter?*

Mbuâ appeared to answer the chief's question:

— *They gave you a bone to keep. Where is it?*

— *I ate it,* it replied, shamelessly, and even with a snap of the jaws!

— *Well,* said the chief, *you will eat only bones, as you like them so much!*

— *I don't kill anyone who comes up against me!*

To which the chief replied:

— *Didn't you see anyone last night?*

— *Yes, I did!*

— *So how many did you kill?*

— *None.*

— *So what are you complaining about, and what have you come to ask me?*

The chief raised his court, which didn't need to deliberate: the plaintiffs had sentenced themselves!

M'Sônghi Lumpfîkini and Ngô

M'Songhi[3] caught a bat at the foot of a palm tree.

[3] – M'Songhi = Palm wine collector (Harvest)

— *I will kill it and feed it to my starving children!*

And he slammed it three times against the trunk of the palm tree.

— *I beg you to let me live!* begged the little birdlike and mouselike creature. *Perhaps I will be useful to you one day!*

M'Sônghi, who was a good-natured person, released Lumpfîkini, who flew away and disappeared into the forest. As time went by, it lost all memory of it.

One hot day Ngô came to M'Sônghi's house to quench its thirst. But it refused to drink from the small gourd offered to it by the generous M'Sônghi:

— *I only drink in it,* said Ngô, who took out a human skull from its bag!

And it had itself served a drink there!

Ngô drank so much and so well that at the end hiccups of satisfaction shook it.

Then it remembered all its human victims and, with a visibly happy face, it congratulated itself:

— *Nine human heads I have already eaten, the tenth will be today!*

This statement, which had the value of a confession, or a threat, and the unusual sight of the human skull where Ngô had just drunk, made M'Sônghi shudder with terror and believe that his last hour had arrived!

But Lumpfîkini arrived at once. It too refused to drink from the small gourd handed to it by M'Sônghi. It takes out of its bag a skull of Ngô, and, the word accompanying the gesture, it declares:

— *I never drink anything but from it!*

Lumpfîkini drank, so much so that at the end hiccups of satisfaction. The memory of all its feline victims came back to its mind and, with a visibly happy face, it congratulated itself:

— *Nine Ngô heads I have already eaten, the tenth will be today!*

Lumpfîkini hadn't yet finished speaking when Ngô ran off without asking for its rest.

Mbuâ
Na Mbûma

Mbûma asked Mbuâ:

— *Of you or of me, which of us does the master hold in higher esteem?*

Mbuâ answered it bluntly:

— *It's me! And unquestionably!*

— *You're mistaken, it's me!*

— *Is that right? It isn't true! Open your eyes, open your ears, you will see the evidence! For, tell me, what services are you doing for your master? You don't hunt for him; you run around the whole house all day, and with you fed doing nothing! Is it the little mice you catch that feed your master? If he ate any of them, the news would explode in the whole village. He would be the laughing stock of the whole village! I, on the other hand, am entirely devoted to the service of my master: you see me leaving every morning in his company for the hunt. My loins strongly marked by the bell that is continually attached to them. But I don't say that I complain of so much trouble, considering that the main thing for me is to provide for my master. And no hunting if I'm absent! Then, my friend, wouldn't you give all your esteem to one who brings you so much good?*

— What esteem? Because you go hunting for little genets, you think you have acquired or conquered a marked preference from your master! I think I can say that my master likes me very much. For good reason: the day before yesterday I caught and put out of action a fine mouse which was about to take away a garland of eels, and my master would have fasted!

But this is only one example of a thousand, whereas you mention pieces of game that are never seen! However, and I grant you this, if it's true that you're more esteemed than I am, our master is just the person to decide between us, and to prove it!

For that purpose, let us both go up to sleep in his bed: we shall know, when he sees us there, which of us he loves more.

— *Let's go,* replied Mbuâ.

When we've agreed, so soon as we've done it. Here are our two gamblers in their master's bed!

The latter didn't even notice them before he got angry, but it was Mbuâ which was the one he was particularly angry with:

— *Get out of here, and as fast as you can, with your ticks!*

The master doesn't mince his words, and he beats Mbuâ with a stick, who jumps off the bed and runs away screaming in pain.

Mbûma chuckles and laughs:

— *Well? Well? Whom does the master esteem?*

It's to take revenge that the dogs have been fighting the cats since.

Mbôma Na Nchiêchié

They lived together. Mbôma had five children, and Nchiêchié also had five. But Mbôma ate its children.

— *Add me to my children,* said Nchiêchié,

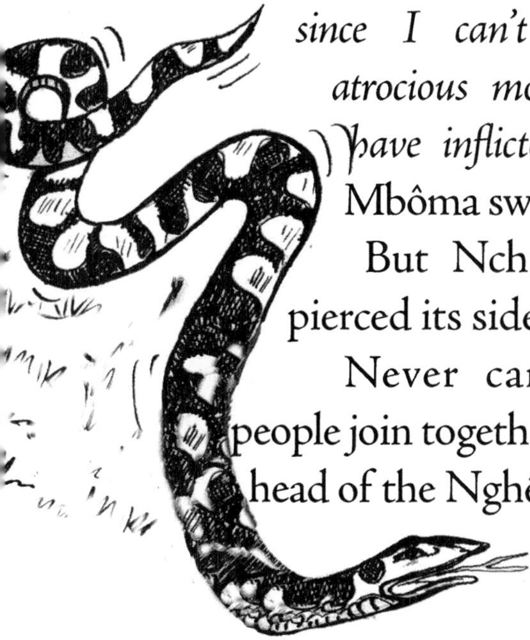

since I can't survive the atrocious mourning you have inflicted on me.

Mbôma swallowed.

But Nchiêchié horns pierced its sides, and it died!

Never can two clever people join together to cut off the head of the Nghêmbo!

Nchiêchié
Nzôbo na Nkûmbi

On the way to a consultation with a fetishist, Nchiêchié came across a market. They were trading in peanuts, which were doing very well. Nchiêchié wanted to sell some peanuts. It turned around and went to find Nzôbo:

— *I know a market where peanuts are highly valued. As I know that you have a lot of them, I will set up a stall there. It's to ask you to go there together that I have come to see you.*

Nzôbo accepted the proposal, and Nchiêchié fixed the day of the next market. But it had no peanuts! It loaded a bag with coals and carefully covered it with rags. On the agreed day, Nchiêchié went to wait for Nzôbo at the place of their meeting. When it saw it coming, it claimed to have a stomach ache, and rolled on the ground, moaning:

— *Ayi! My stomach is cramping and I'm dying of pain! But if you go to the river to get me some water, I will feel better.*

Nzôbo takes a bottle and runs to the river. But behind it, Nchiêchié exchanges its coals for its companion's peanuts, then lies down on its stomach and makes a thousand faces. Nzôbo brings it a drink. After a while, Nchiêchié says:

— *I feel a little better. Now we can walk slowly to the market.*

But when they get there, Nchiêchié asks to sell its peanuts first, and quickly it has sold its whole bag. Opening its bag in turn, Nzôbo was astonished to find that it was full of coals! The whole market was angry:

— *What? Have you got such, a cracked head that you come to sell us coals instead of peanuts? What are you doing to the reputation of our market?*

Ashamed, Nzôbo tried in vain to run away. We catch it! And we kill it for you.

Nchiêchié returns to its village, rich and without remorse.

On the way, it meets Nkûmbi:

— *Ah, my friend, I've just come back from a market where the peanut trade is going well!*

Nkûmbi house is full of peanuts bags. Nkûmbi wants to know about this market and go there.

— *Never mind!* Nchiêchié reassures it and sets the day of the next market.

It repeated its trick of malice. But Nkûmbi had hidden a fetish statue in its bag. When Nchiêchié wanted to take its peanuts, the fetish shouted at it:

— *What do you want to do there?*

Nchiêchié was very ashamed, and its dark plan failed. At the market, Nchiêchié was booed when it unpacked its bag of coal:

— *So it was you who deceived Nzôbo! You will suffer the same fate as it.*

Nchiêchié seized and put to death.

Mfûlu
Na Mbuâ

It's mango season. Mfûlu is elated, because she has made mangoes, its favourite treat. Every morning, at dawn, it's at the foot of the mango trees, picking up the fruits that fell during the night.

Poor Mfûlu! It doesn't know how to climb. And the mango trees don't belong to her! Some days, the mangoes fall on her head or on her back when it's windy. But it can't complain, let alone cry out. It's afraid of attracting the owners' attention.

The trees aren't its. Only she knows what it's enduring in its soul. This is a lot of its life every morning now...

One morning, as it's on its way to pick mangoes, Mfûlu meets Mbuâ:

— *Good morning, sister Mfûlu! Where do you go like this every morning, early in the morning? And when you come back home, it's with a round belly, and your bag is always swollen! Do you know some secret place where you go to all the time?*

— *Well, I go down to the lower part of the village to pick mangoes.*

— *Give me two!*

— *There is no shortage of mangoes at the foot of the mango trees, and they're lying around, rotting on the spot. So you can go and stock up on them, as you like, as you can.*

And there's no way I will give you the ones I've picked up, even if you resurrect my mother who died a long time ago. Finally, and to tell you the truth, I don't expect you to bury me when I die!

— Ho my goodness! So much talk for two mangoes! Will you never be hungry again when you eat your mangoes?

— Come with me, I'll show you where I pick them; you won't say I have a bad heart!

— Come on, I'll follow you.

— Yes, but on one condition!

— What condition?

— That you don't scream even if a mango falls on your head!

— I understood, I'm not deaf.

Mbuâ and Mfûlu take the path of the mangoes. They litter the ground at the foot of the mango trees. They collect so many that they have to make bags with palms to carry them. But then the wind starts to blow. Many mangoes fall from the trees. Mbuâ receives one, then two, then three, on its head, without saying a word, but at the fourth mango, it cries out in pain!

— Ayi! My mouth!

— *Hush! Shut up! The village is very close, and we risk they beat us!*

As Mfûlu spoke in this way, some men came running. Mbuâ, seeing them coming, throws its mangoes and flees. It's pursued, but it can't be caught. In turn, Mfûlu wants to flee, but being low on her feet, it's quickly caught.

— *Ah, so it's you who comes to collect our mangoes! We may come every morning, but when we arrive, there isn't a single mango left at the foot of the mango trees. And in your place, we suspected the women who pass by here, on their way to their plantations! But as you have eaten our mangoes, we will eat you too.*

With that, Mfûlu is taken to the village where it's locked up in a basket. The next day, the people of the village go hunting. They ask a child to look after Mfûlu:

— *Watch over her,* they tell him; *we're going into the forest; we will eat her on the way back, with palm nut sauce.*

Having said this, they leave. A few moments later, Mfûlu asks the child:

— *Did you understand what your fathers told you?*

The child answers:

— *Yes, I understood well.*

— *What did they tell you?*

— *To watch over you until the evening, when they will come to eat you with palm nut sauce!*

— *I knew it! You didn't understand well, because they told you to go and dunk me in the water! That way, when they eat me in the evening, they will find my flesh tender!*

Naïve, the child takes Mfûlu out of the basket, takes her by the arm, and goes to the river to immerse her. And when it's in the water, it tucks its head and legs into its carapace, then plays dead! The child frightened by this:

— *Poor Mfûlu is dead! They're going to beat me tonight.*

He turns it repeatedly, but it remains motionless. Thinking of the blows it will receive, the child bursts into tears. It leaves the river, leaving Mfûlu behind, and returns to the village.

— *Well done,* says Mfûlu who sinks and disappears into the water.

But, still worried, the child returns to the river, goes back into the water, steps on a stone, and thinks it has stepped on Mfûlu! He carries it to the village where he arrives as the people returning from the hunt. When they see the child with the stone, they cry out:

— *Where did you put Mfûlu that you were told to guard?*

— *I went to the river to dip it in water to soften its flesh, but as it can't stand, water, it's dead!*

— *Your foolishness is beyond measure. It's only matched by your naivety!* You say to the child you keep blaming. *Didn't you know that Mfûlu lives in water, and that this is its usual environment? If your father continues to make children of your kind, it's to spoil the country! You're like some legendary record holders of stupidity: when they were sent to collect palm nuts, they brought back thorns! So, instead of Mfûlu, you will make us eat a stone! Don't wait until you have a beard and white hair to become intelligent!*

While the child was being harshly chastised, Mfûlu had returned to its home. Squatting Mbuâ was waiting for it. It expressed its dissatisfaction:

— *Because of you, I almost became a victim of men. Fortunately, my intelligence and the naivety of a child saved me! But I swear that from this day on I will flee your company, on the strength of your ever-running nose!*

Ngô Tchibûbu na Mpâdi

Their companions gave birth the same day. They said to each other:

— *Our stomachs are throbbing; we must eat meals with palm nut sauce; in this way, our udders will swell and overflow with milk for the good health of our young.*

Ngô female said to its companion:

— *I'm dying to eat palm nuts. You go and get me some.*

The other two companions expressed the same desire to their companions. Ngô went in search of the nuts, but grumbled:

— *My companion will push me to go and steal! It's too greedy, and has a gluttonous appetite!*

Mpâdi went off in search of nuts, cursing its companion's outrageous demands:

— *It's the women who risk causing famine one*

day and, although we have enough to eat at home, we must have nuts at all costs!

But at Tchibûbu house, the atmosphere is tense. Its companion doesn't mince words, and it threatens.

— *Nuts! I have to eat nuts today, or I'll get a divorce!*

— *You mustn't use nuts as a pretext for divorce if you want to leave,* says Tchibûbu, grumbling. Then heads for the forest to get some nuts.

Ngô meets Tchibûbu, who mutters in annoyance at the foot of a palm tree. Mpâdi soon meets them there and asks them what they have come to do together in the forest:

— *Are you looking for Nkûmbi or palm worms?*

— *Alas! No! Our women want to eat palm nuts at all costs today! So we have been beating the forest since the morning...*

— *Oh, this nut story!*

Mpâdi feels sorry for its companion. It too wanted to eat nuts, whatever the cost! But it's an epidemic!

— *Then we're in the presence of a plot,* declares Ngô: *our companions acted together!*

— *Our presence here for the same purpose leads me to believe you,* Tchibûbu adds.

— *Complicity, consultation, or connivance, that's all well and good,* ironies Mpâdi, *but it's in vain that I wander all over the forest: not a shadow of a nut!*

Ngô tells it about all the trouble it and its companion went through before arriving at the foot of this palm tree loaded with three bunches of nuts.

But it hastens to add:

— *We're still far from the end of our troubles, because, although the nuts are ripe, we can't pick them. As we don't know how to climb! So we're here waiting for the ones that the birds can drop, to pick them up.*

But Mpâdi says it's an excellent climber:

— *Give me a cut-cut!*

Here is Mpâdi at the top of the palm tree:

— *Out of the way! I will drop the first diet.*

— *No,* says Tchibûbu, *don't let it fall to the ground: the nuts will scatter; but rather throw it in my direction, I will intercept it in its fall.*

Mpâdi dropped the three bunches and Tchibûbu intercepted them all, without losing a nut.

— *Come down now; we will extract the nuts, unless each of us wants to take a bunch and carry it all to the village.*

— *How can we carry a whole bunch of nuts with all their prickles?* Said Ngô; *Isn't it more convenient to put the nuts in a bag of branches?*

— *You speak well. Can someone get them out for us?*

But Ngô dismisses this concern:

— *Why did God give me long nails? Don't worry, I'll take on the task.*

— *Yes, but who will preside over the sharing?*

— *The question doesn't even arise. Once again, am I not there? Only, we don't have enough leaves to wrap up the slices.*

Tchibûbu offered to go and pick them:

— *Wait for me a moment, I'll go and get them.*

But as it crept through the trees, it said to itself:

— *I can see that these nuts will lead to trouble. Ngô presides and shares. The palavers, the outcome of which would only be beneficial to it, is to be feared, as our fellow man isn't naturally sociable. I, for example, will I even have three nuts, as long as we start by looking, for leaves to put them on? So, my friends, if you see me again, it will be a devil, but not me!*

That said, Tchibûbu simply takes the road to the village.

— *What happened to him?* Ask the other two.

Waiting in vain. So Mpâdi went in search of Tchibûbu. But on the way, the same thoughts came to his mind as Tchibûbu:

— *It's common knowledge that Ngô is full of wickedness; it uses the right of the strongest, and it wouldn't surprise me if it took all the nuts! So, I might as well tell it to take them; it hasn't cut off my arms, if I have to go and get the nuts elsewhere at all costs.*

Mpâdi didn't return, and continued on the way to the village. Ngô was afraid, in its turn, and thought that it was a plot against it:

— They are too cunning to allow anything untoward to happen to them. Neither intelligence nor strength is lacking in Tchibûbu or Mpâdi, which catches bunches of nuts in flight without the slightest scratch! I will go home instead of risking my life for nuts!

Leaving the three bunches at the foot of the palm tree, Ngô went home, worried.

But in the evening, gathered together, they asked each other:

Tchibûbu: *when I went to fetch the leaves, I was afraid that Ngô might use the law of the strongest to share the nuts. It was better for me to give it up.*

Mpâdi: *in turn, I had the same idea, fearing to leave my skin for nuts. Too bad for my companion!*

Ngô: *left alone in the forest, I was worried; I thought of a nasty trick by Mpâdi and Tchibûbu. They would gang up on me to prevent me from getting my share of the nuts!*

The mutual distrust of the three companions provoked bursts of laughter in the whole village. The women did not get any nuts, but that was all it took for their companions to get to know each other better!

Ngô, Nkûmbi Na Mâma'ù[4]

Ngô and Nkûmbi lived in the same village, each in its neighbourhood. One day, Ngô visited Nkûmbi. To honour its visitor, Nkûmbi slit the throat of a goat from which it only removed the guts, and prepared it in a large pot. It let it simmer, and came to speak with its friend:

— *My brother, it's a great honour that you do me by coming to see me today. Shall the spirits have dictated this noble move to you? But if only I had known you were coming! Only yesterday I had a good calabash of palm wine, although no one helped me to drink it. So, the old saying goes: it's wise to keep the remains of a meal, because you never know the day that you will be honoured with a visit! And here I'm, caught off guard! But I cook some cassava leaves which, for want of a better word, will serve us well as a meal.*

After this courteous introduction, the two friends chatted freely, talking about the rain and the weather, while the big pot sang on the fire.

4 – Leopard, Lerot and their Mum

It was time for the meal:

— *I'm obliged,* says Nkûmbi, *to serve the meal myself, because all the children have scattered into the bush, either to hunt birds, to set traps for rats, or to fish.*

Having said that, it leaves for the cooking pot. Left alone, Ngô muttered:

— *Cassava leaves spoil your teeth; who will eat them? It's a dish for the poor. But, in order not to appear proud, I must be satisfied with it.*

Nkûmbi brought the whole pot, at the sight of which Ngô exclaimed:

— *Whoa! You! You' re going to make bellies flow!*

Its host reassured it:

— *Don't let the size of the pot impress you. I'm serving the meal in the pot, because there are no plates.*

But when it saw the real contents of the pot, Ngô couldn't contain its joy: its lips opened in a wide fan, revealing gluttonous fangs.

— *Brother Nkûmbi knows how to tempt and test people's hearts! I thought it was a real plate of cassava leaves! After all, it isn't a bad dish. I would have missed a good meal, however, if I had shown any distaste for it! But with you, one must understand the opposite of what you mean.*

— *It's the nature of friends to understand each other half-heartedly. So start by sharpening your teeth with good meat, while I go and see if the women have a piece of cassava bread.*

Ngô is voracious. It has already eaten half the big pot. When it dips its hand in, it takes a whole leg of goats and stuffs it in its mouth! When Nkûmbi comes back with cassava, there is only one piece of meat left at the bottom of the pot! But Ngô will play the smart guy:

— *Little Brother Nkûmbi, return the cassava to where you took it. Because the women are intractable: when they come back in the evening, dizzy from the sun from their plantations, they attack the people who have stayed in the village.*

Nkûmbi takes it at its word and goes to return the cassava. When it returns, Ngô has finished emptying the pot, licking the inside of it, and, satisfied, declares:

— *The ancients had a thousand reasons for saying that the day the poor find food, the rich die of hunger! By that I mean that without you my guts would be shrinking today.*

As Ngô spoke thus, it was seized with a big hiccup, which made it say:

— *When one has eaten, and eaten well, one must belch; otherwise one is only a miser!*

It added:

— *Yes, I have eaten well, and I'm full. But sit down, I'll tell you what's on my mind. You know that all the animals in the bush are afraid of me. So I wonder why they would want me to believe that I'm not only naughty, but really awful! But, you, with whom I live in the same village, can you tell me if you have heard that Brother Ngô has gone to cause trouble somewhere? When I'm not attacked first, I'm fine with anyone, anyone at all. And, by what you have just done, you have shown how we must live together, in good understanding. Yes, when a visitor comes to the door of your house, you must be happy, you must do everything to make it happy. So you and I, as we're today, have sealed a friendship until death…*

— *May it be so, and for ever!* Nkûmbi approved.

After which, Ngô took leave of, its friend:

— *Brother Nkûmbi, later, when we part, I will go to sleep. If anyone hears from me again, it will be tomorrow.*

Many days passed. Ngô returned to Nkûmbi.

— *How is Brother Ngô doing?*

— *We're well, and at your home!*

— *We have nothing to complain about.*

— *Thank the gods for that! But I have come to make you a proposal.*

— *Ah! And what is that?*

— *Our mothers are all full of fat, they look like fat crickets. Can't we cook them? The continuation would be very interesting for us!*

Nkûmbi accepted the proposal:

— *Is that a problem? However, I agree that we should first eat your mother, who is now, in everyone's opinion, too fat. I'm even afraid that it will soon choke on its fat. As for my mother, it still has to earn a little bacon, and we will have plenty of time to eat it.*

Ngô returned to his neighbourhood and began to pester his mother, asking her to give him food:

— *Hunger is torturing me; give me something to shut it up quickly!*

— *Wait a moment, the pot is still on the fire; I'll soon take it off.*

— *I won't wait, or I'll smash your pot to bits!*

Mother Ngô reproaches it:

— *The way you're always crying out for food, make sure you don't steal one day! Since you came back from your hunts, has there been a single time that you have given me even one little rat! But what motherly heart can remain unforgiving? Wait a moment, I'll serve you some food...*

A hungry stomach has no ears! Ngô gets angry and pounces on its mother, who begs it to let it go. But it's as if it's talking to a deaf man, and it dies by strangulation! Ngô cuts it into pieces which it cooks under the ashes, and goes to call Nkûmbi:

— *Come! My mother cooks under the brazier, but let's hurry up, because the fire is gradually dying out under the fat, and all the embers are sizzling! Ho! What a feast are we going to have?*

Nkûmbi withdrew for a moment with its children to ask them to go and extract some latex in the nearby forest, and to bring it to the village, after having transformed it into rubber. The children left, and Nkûmbi went to Ngô house where it made a very good meal.

It said to its friend:

— *We would eat next Sunday, my mother; but I think that is still too far away, and I fear that by then it will die of illness. So we'll eat it tomorrow; don't forget to come.*

Back in its neighbourhood, Nkûmbi feigns a quarrel with its mother. In its false anger, it beat a banana tree trunk with a club. Amazed, Ngô thought that Nkûmbi was killing its mother!

— *What good food, and what a feast tomorrow!* It said to itself.

Nkûmbi cut into pieces the big rubber ball brought from the forest by its children. It built a fire and cooked the pieces of rubber under the ashes. Ngô arrived in a hurry at Nkûmbi house.

— *I was expecting you,* said Nkûmbi, *and you're a little late. My mother was too fat, not to die before Sunday. So I did well to kill it right away.*

Ngô licked its lips. Nkûmbi sent one of its children to serve the meal, asking it to take great care:

— *Be very careful, and make sure you don't drop anything!*

Nkûmbi had indeed coated each piece of rubber with oil.

When it served it the first piece, the oil spilled into Ngô hands:

— *It must not slip through my fingers!*

And it swallowed the whole piece. Ngô burned its tongue, but it swallowed the second piece with the same voracity, and almost choked on the third. Its stomach burned, and digestive disturbances plagued it. It sweated. Feeling faint, it got up and staggered towards its neighbourhood. When it arrived home, Ngô died of indigestion!

Ngô
Na Mfûlu

One day, Mfûlu says to Ngô:

— *Let's go and cultivate a field of cassava!*

Ngô answered it:

— *This season, I have no desire to work. I have a feeling that I will die soon.*

Mfûlu went to work alone in the field. But, at harvest time, Mfûlu companion shared the cassava with Ngô companion, without Mfûlu making the slightest objection or the slightest allusion.

The following year, Mfûlu again invited Ngô to go and work with it in the cassava field. This time again, Ngô put forward the same pretext:

— *I wonder if this year will even leave me alive. What's the point of working again?*

Mfûlu went to work alone in the field. But, at harvest time, Mfûlu companion shared the cassava with Ngô companion, without the slightest objection or the slightest hint from Mfûlu.

One day, torn by hunger, Ngô companion went to steal cassava tubers from Mfûlu fields, and Mfûlu companion caught it in the act. The latter ran to warn its husband, who immediately went to its field. Mfûlu said to the thief:

— *If I tell your companion to come and work with me, it never wants to, and you, its beloved, come to maraud in my fields! But I don't want to betray you to your companion or bring you to justice. I will only ask you to erase all your traces in my fields; if you leave them there, how will I know if other Ngô don't come to plunder me?*

Ashamed, Ngô beloved complies. But, as it erased the traces, they reappeared behind it! The poor Ngô beloved had to spend the whole day in Mfûlu fields, for its task was in every way like that of the Danaids sentenced, in the underworld, to pour water eternally into a bottomless vase! Ngô was astonished not to see its companion return until the evening. It had to go looking for it. It found it very busy covering its tracks.

— *What has happened to you that is so extraordinary, it asks it that you're still not thinking of going home?*

But it's Mfûlu who answers it:

— *Your female came to steal in my field. I didn't want to shame her in front of you. Even less, to drag her before a court of justice.*

I asked her to erase all traces of her from my field; after that, it would be free, and I would know from now on if the other Ngô didn't come to steal my cassava tubers. And your beloved is erasing its traces!

— *It's not the end of the world!* Said Ngô, who

pointed out to its female that it was too slow to erase its traces.

Then Ngô comes to its beloved rescue. But as there are now two of them at work, the tracks multiply behind them! Soon, their trampling filled all the field...

Mfûlu felt apologetic for them. It says to them:

— *Stop! You can't erase your traces, because by erasing the first ones, you leave, new ones behind you! You should have thought of that! But if I subjected you to this impossible test, it's to teach you not to come back to maraud in my fields!*

In conclusion, Mfûlu remarked to Ngô:

— *For two years now you have always felt that your death was imminent, and you're still alive! But if you had come to work with me, as I asked. Would your female, have flown?*

Tchîula Na Ngômbulu

They lived together. One day, as it was walking in the forest, Tchîula saw at the top of a tree some fruit bats. They were swaying there like fruit bunches at the end of their stalks. It went to call its friend Ngômbulu:

— *Come, follow me; in the forest near here, I saw some fruit bats; let's go kill them.*

Ngômbulu took its rifle. Tediously, Tchîula led its friend to the foot of the fruit bats tree. Ngômbulu fired. But it was a clumsy hunter and, with each shot, the fruit bats flew away.

— *Pass me the gun,* said Tchîula.

— *Do you think you're more skilful than me?* Replied Ngômbulu.

It passed it the gun anyway. Tchîula is a good shot with a gun. It killed a lot of fruit bats.

In the village, Ngômbulu grabbed all the fruit bats it gave to its female to cook. When it was time to eat them, Tchîula had to settle for a dish of eggplants. It complained bitterly:

— *I'm the one who killed the fruit bats, but it's to eat them with my eyes!*

Another time, Tchîula went into the bush. It entered a thicket at the foot of a mountain. It noticed the presence of hedgehogs, judging by the grass cut everywhere by the herbivores. Tchîula made its way through the thicket. The path had to climb the side of the mountain. At the end of the path, at the top of the mountain, it fixed a large stone. Then it ran to the village to call Ngômbulu:

— *Come, follow me; I have spotted some hedgehogs; let's go and kill them.*

When they reached the path at the bottom of the mountain, Tchîula said to Ngômbulu:

— *Stay here on the lookout, while I go up and bring the hedgehogs down.*

Having climbed to the top of the mountain, Tchîula detached the large stone that it had fixed to it, and let it roll.

— *Watch out!* Shouts Tchîula. *The game is up and coming towards you! Put yourself well in the path to catch it!*

With its lips curled up, revealing all its teeth, Ngômbulu blocks the passage. But the big stone that rolls down the slope breaks its jaws!

Happy to have taken its revenge, Tchîula quietly returns home!

A father tested by his son

A child claimed to be smarter than his father:

— *If I disappeared,* he told him one day, *you wouldn't know where to find me!*

At first the father thought his son was delirious. But later he had to change his mind and convince himself otherwise: the child disappeared in the form of a peanut. A rooster was seen with the peanut in its beak. They wanted to catch it, but the rooster disappeared into the forest. The weasel, who was starving in the forest, chased the rooster.

Attracted by the desperate cries of the bird, the men ran into the forest. The weasel ran away from the hunters. Deep in a thicket, it ate the rooster. But it didn't have time to digest it, because a boa hunting in the thicket caught it in its rings and gobbled it up. The men, still chasing the weasel, came across the boa and clubbed it.

In the village, the boa was butchered; they found the weasel in the belly of the long reptile. They disemboweled the weasel and found the rooster. The rooster was skinned; they found the peanut, and from the peanut came a young man. The father recognised his son.

When he saw this, he was indignant, considering his son's behaviour as an offence:

— *My child! To do this to me! What does he want me to see? I'll prove to him that I saw the sun before him!*

But after thinking about it, the father was indulgent. He said to himself:

— *Isn't it to show me that he's already a man that my son has acted in this way? In that case, it's time I found him a daughter to marry.*

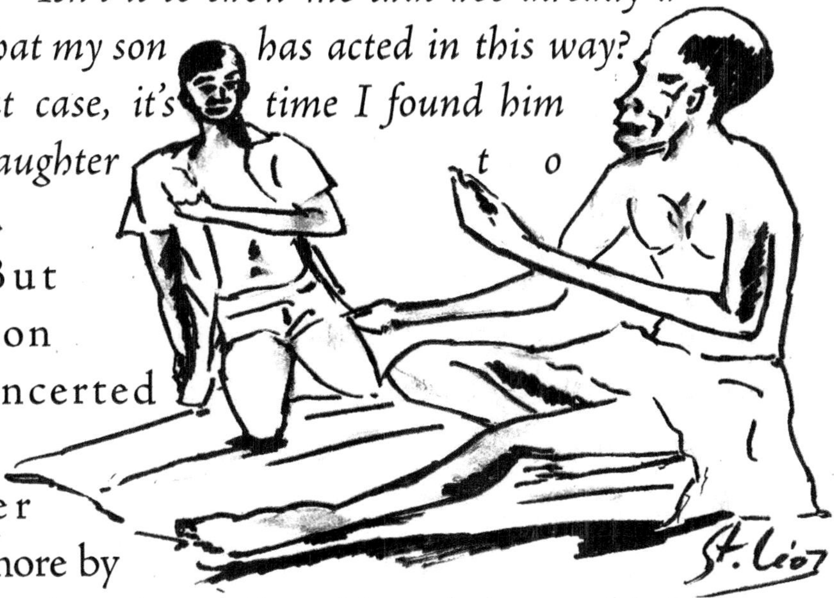

But the son disconcerted the father even more by his refusal to take a wife, although he would choose the most beautiful, and from a respectable family.

Old men are wise, and the father let time do its work...

One day, however, the father decided to resolve the crisis:

— *Take the gun,* he said to the child, *we're going hunting.*

They set off. When the dog was let go, a boar came running. Bang! The father fired, and the animal collapsed.

— *Run to the village,* said the father of the child, *and take the bag left in the house.*

When the child arrived at the village entrance, he was surprised to hear crying:

— *What has happened to us?* He asks himself, his heart pounding; *we have hardly left the village for an hour, and no one is sick...*

But when he entered the house, he was even more surprised to see his father dead, lying at full length on his deathbed, covered with a shroud!

— *It's impossible,* says the bewildered child, *my father has stayed in the forest; he himself sent me to fetch his bag; he can't be dead! No!*

Confused, he returned to the forest where his father, who was still waiting for him, began to berate him:

— *How? I send you to get the bag, and you come back empty-handed!*

The son wants to speak, but the father cuts him off:

— *Go and get it quickly!*

But in the village, the crying continues around the dead man! The child doesn't understand anything any more. Is it a hallucination in daylight? No, because the people of the village, whose crowd has grown since the beginning, start to chastise him harshly:

— *What? Your father is dead, and you're walking around!*

The child doesn't know what to do:

— *It's impossible! I went hunting with my father just an hour ago! He killed a boar, and it's on his orders that I'm coming back to get the bag he left at home! But I'm coming! And what do I see? The corpse of my father! But when I go back to the forest, I find him alive! I don't have two fathers, one of whom is dead, while the other is still alive!*

The child returned to the forest. The father was still there, waiting for him:

— *What's the matter with you? And where is the bag?*

— *What is happening to me is something no one in the world has experienced: in the village you're dead and everyone is crying over you, but here you're alive! What does that mean?*

And the child burst into tears.

The father laughed.

— *You're stronger than me! So understand today that parents, who have seen a river or an ant first, don't need their children to show them.*

The beard, they say, doesn't make the wise man.

Not all old people are fools. Nor are all young people geniuses!

Kûti Na Ngûndum'nua

The party was in full swing among the birds. They had come from all over the world, from all skies and all continents. It was a real parade.

Mbêmba, clad in an ashen-grey jacket, proudly displayed its royal livery. Lumbûé hovered casually over the jubilant crowd. The Kitômbo and the Martinets, in their colourful blue silk and white outfits, stretched their beaks to the wind, to which the festival seemed to add length. All the Wading birds, perched on their long poles, strutted up and down, wiggling their long-necked beaks. Bidukiâ and Ndingâ were cooing, simpering like bridesmaids. Mâ Tchâku and the Toucans seemed driven by their hooked mandibles, like gables on a street.

Bâ Nkêlele and the Peacocks, opening their tails in a fan shape, were doing a cartwheel. Bâ Nsûsu, with their poppy-coloured crest, had a martial leg. They arrived, preceded by their delegations, in groups, according to their kinship links, and according to their regions. All this world, from the barnyard and aviary birds, through the Paradise and Fly Birds, the Cranes, the Toucans, the Hornbills, the Flamingos and the Pelicans, to the tiny Ntiêtié, were mad with joy, punctuated by the rumbling of drums.

Dragging its frock coat, the colour of mourning, Kûti was the last to arrive at the place of the fraternal agape, made late by Ngûndum'nua who asked it to bring it to the feast, under its cover:

— *I'm too small to go alone, it said to it, and I'm very much afraid of getting lost amid this raging winged kind! But perhaps I could also be useful to you in some way.*

Kûti agreed to the prayer, took the sparrow in its mourning-coloured frock coat pockets, grumbling a bit, and made a triumphal entrance to the party, very much noticed. It wasn't too late. The final preparations for the banquet were still in progress.

We decided that Mâ Tchâku would ensure the service of order, that the Tsêkosso would enliven the feast with their antlers, the doves would serve the table,

while the marabouts would act as gourmet cook.

All went well, and all the toasts pronounced for the occasion were in honour of the poultry world cordial and sacrosanct understanding...

But the birds had to close the party with the choice of a song that would henceforth be their patriotic anthem. The merit and honour would go to the best composer singer.

Thus, on the theme of Hymn to the Birds, candidates from all walks of life came forward. They presented themselves in turn, in alphabetical order:

Mbêmba trompeta et glatit ;

Nsuêlé margota et carcailla ;
Tchifuândanga cancana et nasilla ;
Nsûsu coquoricota et claironna ;
Munghângha croassa ;
Fiêfié gazouilla ;
Tchindiâmakoko pépia ;
Nguâri cacaba ;
Tchâku soliloqua et bavarda ;
Tchidukiâ gémit...

The jury was disappointed.

But in front of its embarrassment and perplexity, Ngûndum'nua signalled to Kûti to sing.

— *I never knew how to sing,* it whispered in the ear of Ngûndum'nua.

— *Go ahead anyway! I will help you. Just make-believe you're singing, wagging your beak. From your pocket where I'm hiding, I'll sing a beautiful melody!*

Thus reassured, Kûti gets up and says that it wants to try its luck, too. But its candidacy causes either burst of laughter or mocking murmurs:

— *Is it, singing? What can come out of its gloomy, hoarse and sinister voice?*

Ngûndum'nua persisted.

— *Go on! Go on! Count me in!*

The jury took note of the request, and invited Kûti to perform. Kûti readjusted the collar of its mourning-coloured frock coat. It feigned a small cough to disgorge itself; then, followed a small silence which entertained the audience a lot. Ngûndum'nua:

— *I count to three, and you attack! One! And two! And three!*

Kûti opened its beak. What a wonder to hear! The salvoes of applause greeted the first trills. The voice was pure, clear, as clear as the water of a brook, without burr or blunder. Sometimes low, sometimes high, the scores followed one another, linked together, and soon the melody flowed and cascaded on the feast goers bewitched by the charm...

Kûti sang thus, without stopping, with inflections of the voice, and tremolos. When, at last, it stopped, an immense clamour rose from the crowd to give it a standing ovation, and Kûti bent over to say its thanks and its joy. The comments of praise went on, in honour of Kûti who had just revealed its talent of virtuoso. Some called it the Phoenix of the festival; for others, it was Philomena! It was showered with a thousand and one rewards, and the party ended with Kûti triumph. Everyone went back to their homes with joy in their hearts.

Winner of the song, Kûti left, full of fortune. But it kept all the rewards behind it. Claiming that Ngûndum'nua had no right to claim them. For, without it, the sparrow wouldn't have gone to the party and besides, did it have the courage to face the numerous public?

Without any insistence, Ngûndum'nua went home, indignant only that ingratitude was in this world!

But Kûti supposed success had been such that no one forgot it in a hurry and, some time later, the night owl was invited to sing at another festival.

It accepted and left to find Ngûndum'nua, and to ask it to lend it, once again, its good offices, its beautiful voice, with great eagerness:

— *Come on! This time, fortune is ours! I've been invited to sing at another party. We'll do what we did the other day. I'll feign to sing, while you perform your beautiful flights!*

Ngûndum'nua doesn't refuse. And there they went. Like the other time, Kûti hid Ngûndum'nua in one of its mourning-coloured frock coat pockets. It arrives and we celebrate it. But when the time comes to sing, Ngûndum'nua is silent, and Kûti rolls and lowers its big eyes in turn. People are surprised and wonder.

— *What has become of the other day's beautiful voice?*

Risking everything, Kûti finally makes up its mind. But when it opens its beak, the sinister and lugubrious hooting that comes out of it makes everyone flee in panic, and everyone, believing in the announcement of a great misfortune, recommends its soul to the spirits!

Ndûmba Na Ngômbulu

She was the most beautiful in the country, but her parents died when she was only ten seasons old. She had five older brothers and one younger brother. She was very fond of all her brothers, and they, being hunters by profession, had surrounded the house with a high wall to protect their sister during the long hours they were away hunting.

They usually didn't return until the tardy in the evening.

When they arrived at the gate of the wall, the brothers sang a song to announce their return. Recognising the voices, the sister ran to open the door.

The young girl, because she was beautiful, attracted many suitors. Ngômbulu in turn resolved to go and see the girl who said to be the most beautiful in the country! But never had a woman been more difficult to seduce:

— *So far,* it said as it went along, *all the lovers who have tried to win her good graces have had the door shut in their faces, and they have failed! But I, as king, have a good chance of seducing her and reducing her. Especially since I will say to her, thanks to me your brothers bring back the game from their hunts. With all this, she would be tough to keep her door open to me!*

Ngômbulu arrives at the door of the wall; it knocks.

— *Who is there?* The girl asks.

— *It's me, Ngômbulu, king of the animals! It's me also that gives your brothers all the games they bring you in the evening, because I know why they always go hunting.*

The girl replies:

— *Unfortunately, I'm sorry, I can't open the door for you when my brothers are away. But if you want to see me, come back another time, or wait until they return in the evening.*

But Ngômbulu, who doesn't see it that way, takes exception to the girl's intransigent attitude:

— *Why do I have to wait for your brothers when I don't know when they'll be back? Do I have to give up my business today because of your brothers?*

The girl doesn't disarm.

— *Under these conditions, you can leave, and come back another time...*

Ngômbulu went away, cursing the girl's pride:

— *And to think that I'm a king! I postponed my palaver that I was supposed to settle today, only to come and see her, but the beautiful girl laughed in my face, instead of opening her door to me!*

As it spoke, on the way it bumped into a stump:

— *Ayi! Damn you,* it complained bitterly. *Does it give you such pleasure to make someone suffer? Well, I'll rip you out and throw you in the fire!*

The stump begs.

— Grant me your forgiveness, I beg you! Maybe I have some good news for you!

— What good news?

-—If you don't tear me out, I will tell you.

— If you have to talk to me, do it quickly! It's getting darker and I hurry home.

— Well, here's the thing: I don't like women, I'll say it straight. I used to be someone, me you see like that. Women made me unhappy. For nothing, they would run around looking for me. They cut off my arms. Because of them, I no longer have any children.

After ruining me, they ran away from me, to go and impoverish others. I'm so angry with women that I came here to wait for them in the middle of the road, to at least, cut off all their toes. The women? Ah! Tell me about it! They don't even have any respect for the leaders! And you yourself, don't you know anything about where you come from? Isn't it because of a woman that you come home at a late hour?

When I heard you talking earlier, I thought it was a woman coming, and I got up to stand against her! But here it is! Against my will, I almost harmed you! The wise man was right: a fight at night is bad; you think you're hurting an enemy, but it's one of your own! This is what happens to us, you and me! But I must pay for the evil I have done to you, albeit unintentionally. For that you must eat, the girl in question. Without that, my heart can't find peace!

Ngômbulu, astonished as well as interested, asked it:

— *How, or from whom, do you know about this story?*

— *I'm a soothsayer. So it's up to you if you want to get the girl, because I'm a fetishist too. But she's tough to get, because she's very clever. It's enough, however, to know how to imitate the voices of her brothers when they sing in front of the door of the wall, in the evening, when they come back from hunting. You will drink the little fetish here. But to have the little voice of the hunting brothers, you must also swallow a burning coal.*

Its voice transformed and slender, Ngômbulu returned to the girl. At the door of the wall, it sings like its brothers. Amazed, she runs to open the door. She's surprised to see Ngômbulu in the doorway. But the young girl bravely suppresses her initial fright and keeps her composure:

— *Hello, king of the animals! I'm happy to see you again. I knew you would come back. But since I made you go back to the door, I've been apologetic to have hurt you. Come in without further ado! I have prepared some fish for you, and tobacco for you to snuff or smoke after your meal.*

Ngômbulu flattered by the gentle language and stroked its mane to express its gallantry, and it was at the height of its joy when the young girl continued its invitation:

— *Come and eat your fish, and drink the honey gathered for you by my brothers!*

But lions are perverse. Ours, while licking its lips at the idea of the good meal it will make. And the heady honey will get drunk on, has the black intention of eating the young girl, on top of everything else! But it betrays itself, for it says out loud what it thinks down below!

Having heard all this, the girl said to him, full of malice:

— *So you don't love me, and you're talking about going back home!*

Ngômbulu laughs:

— *How naive she can be! I say I'll eat her, and she understands that I'm leaving!*

The girl continues, looking stupid:

— *You didn't come to see me!*

But diamonds, cut diamonds! Ngômbulu believed that the girl was speaking sincerely. So it let itself drawn into the house and sat down to eat. While it was eating, she went into the kitchen where palm oil was boiling in a large pot. When she came back, Ngômbulu had already finished eating.

— *And now come and drink your honey!*

Ngômbulu obediently followed.

— *But,* said the girl, *the honey is up there on the*

rack in a pot. It's heavy, and I can't lift it. So I'll go up on the rack while you stay on the ground. I'll tilt the pot, and you'll just have to open your mouth to gorge yourself!

Ngômbulu holds its mouth open, and the girl pours the whole pot of boiling oil on it! The cat's eyes burst under the boiler, and the mane falls apart! The girl finishes her work with a masterful blow of the axe on Ngômbulu head.

She leaves the house and starts to cry. Her brothers come running:

— *What's the matter with you?*

— *Come in and see the house.*

Ngômbulu was lying on the floor. When the brothers saw this, they too began to cry. But the sister stopped them:

— *I cried with emotion! But you? I killed the monster, I'm now out of danger, safe and sound! Since death has spared me, let's have a party!*

The elder brother said:

— *Our sister has come of age. Let us marry her. But what spouse shall we find for her? Let us look for a man who is of equal strength to her.*

So they sent for all the men of the land and said

— *In hand-to-hand combat, whoever defeats our sister, this one will be her husband.*

No one could overcome the girl.

Someone came forward. He looked as if he had come back from the land of the dead, with a squinty eye and twisted feet. When the girl saw him, she got goose bumps and shivered with disdain:

— *Me? Touch that one!*

But her brothers reasoned with her:

— *What we have decided remains decided. We have made no conditions. Nor did we make any reservation. We have said:*

— *Whoever defeats our sister in hand-to-hand combat, he shall be her husband!*

The sister bowed. When the fight started, the girl was on the ground! The strange foreigner is applauded. When the fight started again, she was on the ground again! More applause, more ovations. Finally, the girl is beaten to the punch.

— *Give me my wife, I'm going home,* says the man.

— *I will never go to that man,* the girl sulked.

Just looking at him made her nauseous. But her brothers persisted.

— This is the man we love and this is the man you need! He's as strong, if not stronger than you. And if anything happens to you, he will be your salvation!

Legends

Ndûmba M'Ziéto

They called her Ndôna. This name, when broken down, could mean: who is she? Ndô-Na?

Some names can sum up an entire destiny!

Ndôna had a complex character, even more difficult than one could say. This became clear when her parents had to find her a husband. Ndôna disappointed them. No suitor was handsome enough or wealthy enough for her. The good people of M'ziéto, steeped in tradition, pitied Ndôna's poor parents.

Yet she wasn't lacking, in success. That is an understatement, for Heaven had provided her with a thousand lures. But success is nothing. It vanishes like smoke in the wind if you don't know how to seize it; if you don't exploit it; if you don't honour it in return. But, better than success, a random favour, it's natural grace that we must speak of, about Ndôna.

Ndô-Na? What is she?

Yet none of her suitors came from the common man! They all came from dignified, distinguished, respectful and venerable families, sometimes wealthy, sometimes virtuous. The very way they presented themselves confirmed their social status. Let's judge:

— *I'm the son of the chief Mvuâma, whose name alone is an advertisement! My father, known to all his wealth...*

Ndôna could have had a thousand reasons for refusing the hand offered to him by the son of Chief Mvuâma, for a body sewn in gold doesn't necessarily hide a heart of gold!

— *I'm N'zîtu's son, whom everyone respects for his wisdom and his attachment to customs...*

Ndôna's parents would have liked nothing better than to form an alliance with probity itself!

— *My uncle is a planter, and his fields cover acres as far as the eye can see. His motto: Honour and Labour...*

Ndôna remained deaf, although her mother was a hardworking peasant!

— *I come from a family of warriors whose bravery, doesn't exclude goodness...*

Ndôna didn't know that only gentle hearts are capable of founding viable homes!

— *My grandfather's name is Mâhonsono, and he's all over the place! He never lacks workers or friends...*

But, what face, what empathy did Ndôna have? The least one can say is that Ndôna seemed made to live in a different world from that of M'Ziéto brave people.

Dignitaries from the country sometimes came to the house of Ndôna's parents, with the aim of obtaining their daughter's hand in marriage. But Ndôna wanted a husband as she imagined him.

Pressed by her parents (marry! Marry! When you're a nut, it's easier to let yourself break [eaten]): many nuts get lost and rot in the dunghill! Ndôna, annoyed, didn't want anyone to talk to her about marriage any more. She withdrew into herself, surrounding herself with an opaque silence. At last, she even ended up fleeing the family home.

The poor parents had to admit defeat by their daughter's obstinacy, and from then on they forbade themselves to make the slightest reference to the question.

Things were to remain as they were until one day what was to happen happened. It was a market day, but not a day like any other, for on that day Ndôna made her choice of a husband. A choice? No! Instead, she threw herself into the arms of an exceptional beauty young person. Ndôna couldn't even explain how the love at first sight happened in her heart. When she saw the handsome boy, she loved him unconditionally.

But Ndôna wasn't alone in falling under the young man's spell. The whole market admired him. They talked about him a lot. Even for a long time, after the market. On the way home, and in the evening at the fireside, because, apart from his fine physical features, Ndôna's man wore new clothes, a hat and the latest shoes...

Ndôna was no less attractive to the foreigner. Moreover, she wasn't lacking in beauty, with her abundant hair, coal black, finely braided, the arch of her breasts, round and full of life, and her well-shaped ankle. The foreigner looked at Ndôna, admired her and loved her.

— *That's how I like a woman to be!*

They observed each other. Then, moved by a

mutual impulse, they drew closer, one to the other, panting. Nothing existed around them any more. They embraced each other, kissed for a long time. Without protocol, without ceremony, the two young people took the oath of the covenant. The happy couple didn't wait for the end of the market to set off on their journey towards happiness...

The two lovers walked briskly and purposefully, chatting happily, their words interspersed with bursts of laughter. They walked on like this for a long time, and Ndôna didn't even notice that the day had declined. At one point, however, she felt uneasy, a physical weakness.

— *Shall we rest for a while?*

— *Yes, my dove. But later, by the river we're approaching, a few more steps and we're there.*

They walked even longer than the young gallant had let on.

— *Here we're at last,* he exulted.

The river flowed peacefully. It came out of a forest and flowed into a green plain. Its waters were clear, and fresh to boot. Ndôna wallowed in it and drank a few clear sips, but her young courtier, didn't let her taste the pleasure of the water for long.

— *We have to leave, the day is getting shorter*

— *Aren't you going to bathe?*

— *I don't want to.*

— *Is our village still far away?*

— *Come on, let's go! You'll see.*

The walk took off again, a long one across the fields and plains. She behind, he in front. They walked and walked. The further they went, the less talkative they became. Nightfall caught them on the way. At that fleeting, twilight hour, the extraordinary news of the day had made the rounds of the thatched cottages in the village of M'Ziéto. Ndôna's parents could hardly believe it, stunned by the unusual nature of the event. What could they be dreaming, for now? Their daughter had once again surprised and upset them. She had taken such a commitment, such a risk, and without their knowledge, and against their will! Ndôna had not only acted in defiance of tradition, she should have delayed, to reflect at her leisure!

But here it is! The incredible and unforeseeable adventure was now being told everywhere!

— *When will we finally arrive?*

Ndôna's voice sounded annoyed and irritating. But the other one cut it short:

— *Walk and follow me instead!*

The sudden change of tone and the silence imposed so curtly, didn't fail to disturb the young woman. She felt a cold shiver run through her body from bottom to top. But instinctively she obeyed and wisely followed, in the shadow of the thickening night, the figure of her man, three quarters of which had been dissipated by the rising mist. And at the bend in the road...

— *Give me back my hat, and take back your lousy hair!*

It was the voice of an invisible being, cavernous to a fault, muffled in the tall grass, but at the same time close to the couple.

Without the slightest hesitation, the man tousled his hair and threw the hat into the darkness, towards the strange voice. Ndôna had shuddered; he turned to her:

— *What would you like to say?*

Ndôna shrugged her shoulders, as if to say: Nothing!

But no sooner had the pair of night owls taken a few steps than another voice, just as cavernous and a little guttural, startled Ndôna.

— *Give me back my jacket, and take back your hard crust of mangy skin!*

Ndôna made an effort to control herself and her fright. She glimpsed a human form in the darkness, but it was horribly ugly! Her companion didn't think twice about it. And threw the jacket towards the shapeless figure. They took a few more steps...

— *My shirt!* Shouted, another voice.

— *Here it is! It's still in good condition, and it's as clean as the day you lent it to me.*

— *Yes, but you kept it longer than we agreed!*

The strange shape disappeared into the night.

— *The nice shirt, the nice jacket, the nice hat, they weren't yours!*

— *That's none of your business,* cut in the other, gradually becoming unrecognisable.

— *But you haven't told me your name yet; what do they call you?*

— *What does it matter? Go on, walk!*

— *Yes, but I'm waiting for you to give me back my trousers, and it's about time!*

— *Who just spoke?*

— *It wasn't me,* replied Ndôna to her companion who had turned towards her.

— *It's me,* rectified a gruff voice. *Give me my trousers and hurry!*

The man unzipped his trousers and let them fall, all the while poorly concealing a long tail like that of a monkey!

— *Ah! There you are, at last! Come on, my shoes!*

— *What about me? My hair!*

— *What about me? My nails! Take yours back, all crooked and horny!*

— *Give me back my beautiful voice! You have deprived me of singing enough pleasure!*

— *What about me? My beautiful teeth! Take back yours, all full of decay that gives you bad breath!*

— *Give me back my youth! Here's your old carcass, cracking with every movement!*

— *And I..., and I..., and I...*

A thousand other voices chorused to claim each of their beautiful eyes, their beautiful face, their beautiful hands, their beautiful legs... Ndôna was stunned. She wept with terror, and a flood of tears flooded her young chest of twenty seasons!

As for the charming man of earlier, he was now a deformed wreck. His voice became more and more nasal and inaudible. His eyes, two gaping, oozing holes; his face disfigured; his body, flaccid, with what was left of his upper limbs extended at the end of long, hooked nails; his mouth, a frightful grin; his teeth, sparse, sharp, and ill-ground! He was unrecognisable!

Ndôna was heartbroken. She felt hopelessly lost, remembering the long journey, the disfigurement, the gradual metamorphosis of her companion, the macabre vision of the diabolical forms, and sank into the darkest despair. She understood why her strange and disturbing lover had no name, or rather, he had one that was common to all his kind: a devil!

Yes, it was a devil, disguised, that Ndôna had loved and wanted to marry! And the devil was there, in bone more than in the flesh. Which was far from an understatement!

Was it the curse or the revenge of disappointed, dishonoured and humiliated parents? But Ndôna thought too late about her dear parents. How she was proving them, right a thousand times over!

She suddenly discovered the horror of her abominable character. She saw and measured the extent of the damage he had done her. But above all she saw how wise, good and noble her parents were. They had led a simple, uneventful life right up to their old age, a life that had earned them a lot of respect and admiration from everyone. They had lived following ancestral traditions. To top it all off, the father and mother had fulfilled their family obligations with dignity.

The father went fishing or hunting in the days when he had a break from his tobacco business. The mother laboriously tended her plantations of manioc, groundnuts, yams and corn. Ndôna never lacked anything. As she never experienced poverty. She was, an only child, and therefore pampered, and therefore the only joy and hope of her parents. They had always been lulled by the legitimate dream of one day seeing their daughter settle and found a home. She would thus continue the family line. For what happens to girls who come of age? They're married, obviously! And this is the time, more than ever, when parents are acutely aware of their responsibilities. It's the moment, more than ever, when they impose their authority (but tenderly) on the child who, through naivety, finds our old new world. For, what is more, can the one who misses his life, start it again? The messes or blunders against life are paid for in cash and are irreparable...

But that's it! To the mirages of life she promised herself to be enchanting, Ndôna had substituted her whims and opposed her decision! Fate is something other than pure chance. One forge and gives oneself one's own destiny...

Ndôna was at this point in her reflections, when she felt a hard elbow on her arm. She shuddered. The man, or rather, what was left of him, triumphantly said:

— *We have arrived!*

Ndôna looked wide-eyed, but she saw nothing that resembled a village of men.

— *Where am I?* She asked herself.

She hadn't yet recovered from her astonishment when an invisible force threw her into an underground, an incomparable and incredible kingdom of darkness! Ndôna felt her legs bend and the ground give way under her, in the grip of her fear. She got goose bumps and her hair stood on end. Her breathing became ragged. Ndôna no longer belonged...

To help her move forward in the darkness, the devil (since he had to be called by his name) took Ndôna, trembling, by the hand, and they went into the darkness. At every step he said to her:

— *Be careful! Here is the grave of your late grandfather; there, that of your late aunt; over there, that of your grandmother; further on, that of..., and that of ....*

So he listed all her deceased ancestors, showing her, their graves, although Ndôna couldn't see them. Her heart was beating wildly as she moved forward mechanically, all troubled and sweating with fear. She was half dead with terror. In panic, her beautiful braids of hair were unravelled. To live for a moment, in this world of desolation and distress, Ndôna had married, its ugliness: a devil in survival, her lips pursed in a frightful rictus...

Suddenly, a commotion came from the depths of the abyss. In a violent wind. A squall with confused noises. The clattering of a thousand metal pieces. The sounds of gongs. The hostile cries of fighting forces confronting each other. It disturbed the heavy, poignant silence that reigned supreme over this dark empire. Ndôna's man was carried away in the confusion. Without knowing how, she found herself face to face with a grandmother shrouded in light. This apocalyptic vision finished traumatising her, but the spectre soon reassured her:

— *Only daughter and beloved of my daughter, my little protégée; go, hasten it! Go as quickly as possible to your parents who are crying over you while you're still alive!*

At that very moment, Ndôna distinctly heard the saddened voices of her parents. Her mother's voice above all:

— *Ndôna, oh, Ndôna, where have you gone all alive?*

The grandmother continued her exhortations:

— *Here, you can only get there in the process of purification once all the human senses have been annihilated!*

Go then, hasten your pace! Take this black powder; use it, if necessary: if your escape is threatened, take care to scatter a little dust behind you, to confuse the enemy. But go! Make haste! I can' t insist enough...

Then the ancestor covered his face and melted

into the darkness. A path of light opened up at the feet of Ndôna who, for a moment, couldn't believe her eyes or her ears. She felt her limbs; she was still alive! She wished she had wings right then and there, and that she could go faster than the wind or even the thought itself. Imagination is a beautiful fool: it makes you daydream instead of taking action! Ndôna had to rely only on her two legs and, despite herself, a frenzied race took her away. Ndôna ran and ran until she was breathless...

But the devil, feverishly set off in pursuit of his advantageously acquired and easy victim. He went, the same way, used the same stratagem, and got himself a hat, a shirt, a jacket, trousers, a pair of shoes, hair, nails, a face, a voice, teeth and a graceful body! He became human again, young, beautiful and elegant.

Ndôna continued her mad race, leaving behind her, from time to time, a trail of black dust, the ancestor's fetish, as she prescribed. More than once, Ndôna lost the direction of the path, only to find it again immediately. She tore her graceful skin on the brambles of the thickets. But she was always going to light as the wind...

— Ndôna, oh, Ndôna, where have you gone, all alive?

When Ndôna finally arrived at the threshold of the family house, all shivering, in rags, sweating blood and water, she fell down dead!

Ya bêto vandiki...
(As in the past)

The cuckoo sang:
Mpfi kiâ nsûsu cuckoo
Mpfi kiâ nsûsu cuckoo[1]

It was barely 7 o'clock in the morning. The pigeons had just crossed Mâ Lêmba field at an almost sonic speed. The field sloped down to the River Hôzi, giving a good view of the village. Thus one could hail Mâ Lêmba from her field for an urgent dispatch, as she was visible there and one could follow her activities.

When the monkeys devastated the corn during the night, the next day Mâ Lêmba could be, heard cursing her cousin with a loud voice. But when these overbearing granivores with their instinctive wisdom made a mess of things at about 4 or 5 p.m., the men took their guns and waded across the River Hôzi.

1 —Somebodies think they hear: *The gallinaceous gizzard, cuckoo!*

It was a real kill and a feast in the village, as three or even five monkey were shot at a time with each shot.

That morning, the River Hôzi shimmered under the timid light that pierced through the trees clumps. Zubâbela[2], Bakelâmio[3] and Nânitelamio[4] agreed to go fishing with the bucket. The little Nkâri-a-buâ[5] and Silâho[6] both decided to follow them, without asking the consent of the older girls who had taken the initiative to go fishing.

How will these two little girls, aged nine and twelve, get there? The solution, as always, is to be on the spot during the first and hard operations. This is a very classic trick played by little girls who were learning about the future life, because you have to know how to struggle to feed yourself. The stories and tales around the fire (at the mazîku or mbônghi[7]) are full of tricks and cunning, and the little ones take advantage of them to learn.

Such fishing sessions require a lot of effort on the part of the girls, and the company of little

---

[2] —Zubâbela = personal name literally meaning: Hated voice.

[3] —Bakelâmio invariably means: Those who keep them (memories, words, etc.) or those who wait.

[4] —Nânitelamio means: To whom shall I tell (the news or the memories?)

[5] —Nkâri-a-buâ: Fallen business or better, bankrupt business.

[6] —Silâho: Stop there!

[7] —Mazîku, Mbônghi = Fireplace and place of conviviality in the village community

girls, doesn't seem necessary. But when you get to the starter of the operations, you find jobs you can do then you can claim a well-earned share.

The three big *mpûmpa*[8]agree to go fishing and make an appointment, while trying not to attract the attention of little Silâho. The latter pretends not to understand anything, but suddenly gets up and gets lost behind the hut; her departure isn't noticed.

She goes to find her friend Nkâri-a-buâ and explains to her:

— You know Nkâri[9]*, Zubâ, yâ*[10] *Mio et yâ Nâni are going fishing with a bucket in the river. They have made an appointment to meet at the foot of the big* m'sâti[11] *at the* m'sâmpa[12] *of Tâ Bitêmo, on the path to the spring. Will you come with me?*

— They will take the m'tete[13]*and pretend to go to the bandâ*[14] *to look for tubers. I followed their explanations and Zubâbela suspected that I understood; she diverted the conversation to confuse me, but too late, I had understood everything.*

[8] —The ones that did the hair of Saint Catherine.

[9] —Nkâri, Zubâ, Mio, Nâni: Refer to the previous page; these are abbreviations of Nkâri-a-buâ, Zubâbela, Nânitelamio.

[10] — Yâ abbreviation of Yâya (older brother/sister).

[11] —M'sâti = Name of a fruit tree.

[12] —M'sâmpa = Landmarks of M'Sônghi, the one who harvests palm wine.

[13] —M'tete = Oblong basket carried by women on their heads.

[14] – Bandâ = Pond.

— So, do we follow them?

— Of course!

— Let's go! Take the two big rice dishes and tie them on the back. We'll go ahead of them on the road to M'Yôkolo[15]. *Then, instead of going fishing, we'll go* kû[16] yâba[17]. *We will start by blocking the small branch of the River Hôzi upstream, then downstream. You!* Go *and get the machetes, which will make the work easier for us.*

No sooner said than done; the two young girls get lost behind the tall grass and go into the forest. With sure steps, they rush towards the place of the big meeting.

— Silâho? If they're there, we will pretend not to see them.

— Of course!

Nkâri walks forward, pushing aside with her hands, the vines and branches that impede their progress. Suddenly she stops!

— What is it? Asks Silâho. *A snake?*

— No!

Nkâri turns towards her comrade and says

[15] —M'Yôkolo = Places set up outside the village of women in the dry season for the preparation of cassava.

[16] – Kû = To.

[17] —Yâba = Action of emptying ponds to catch fish.

softly, holding the index finger of her right hand over her mouth while her left hand points towards the river:

— *They're already here!*

— *How do you know?* Silâho asks in a low voice.

Nkâri, with her index finger still in her mouth, points with her left hand to a freshly torn tree branch; it's them. Silâho advises her comrade to move forward without speaking. The two mischievous girls continue on their way, and soon voices can be heard. Zubâbela and Nânitelamio are there...

The two girls stop and ask themselves whether it's better to introduce themselves or change the route so that we're only seen at the river. But soon the sound of brushing leaves grows in volume behind them. By the time they realise it's too late, Bakelâmio has already seen them and cries out loudly:

— *Ah, ah, ah! The clever ones! Where are you going? What are you looking for around here?*

— *Bakelâmio, the two little girls shout together, what's the matter with you? What is it all about?*

— *Come and see my dear friends, come and see these little 'pests', come and see these rascals!*

— *But what is it about?* Shouted Zubâbela running up. *Are Silâho and Nkâri here?*

Nânitelamio then asked:

— *Where are you coming from? Where are you going? And what are you looking for?*

No answer. The girls are so stunned that they can hardly breathe. They have no presence of mind.

Zubâbela then said:

— *But speak up! Where are you going? You, Silâho, will be a liar and an indiscreet person. And you, if you're lucky enough to find a husband later, you will be a bad woman, light and with a bad tongue. Answer, where are you going?*

— *I thought so,* exclaimed Bakelâmio, *she was being clever, the little innocent, but she understood everything!*

— *Well, let them go on their way. The river isn't ours, it belongs to God. They can do as they please.*

— *Yes, go away!* Together said Nânitelamio and Zubâbela.

But the two little girls were crying their eyes out.

— *So, you bow your heads and present your necks to heaven to wait for the Holy Spirit!* Bakelâmio threw mockingly at them.

— *They're waiting for the Angel Gabriel in the manner of Toby,* said Nânitelamio.

— *Hm! The time for miracles has passed,* added Zubâbela. *Let's go, they can wait for their miracle!*

And the three young girls set off along the slope of the River Hôzi. They had made some landing net with the m'tete. One of them searched the river upstream with a stick, from bank to bank. Digging deep into the roots that form tunnels where catfish and eels lie. The other two were blocking the current, with their wide seines placed side by side.

From time to time, they would lift these large baskets and bring out tilapia, catfish and eels from the river.

And suddenly, the idea came to them to proceed with the yâba.

— *Say, friends,* said Nânitelamio, *if we were to do the yâba instead, I think we would catch a lot more fish.*

Meanwhile, Silâho and Nkâri were moving slowly.

— *Nâni,* replied Zubâbela, *you're very lazy and you're always changing from one thing to another. You don't like* bvûter[18] *any more and it's* yâba[19] *that's taken over you now! In this case, these two rascals shouldn't have been reprimanded, but rather flattered, since they had machetes and two wide dishes.*

— *I'll go and get them,* exclaimed Nâni.

The two girls listened and looked at each other, smiling. Silâho raised her eyebrows as if to say: *this will bite.*

— *Silâho... hey, é é é é! Silâho hé é é é é!*

In the distance, the echo answered with: ahoy, ahoy, ahoy, ahoy... while Nâni ran up the hill and called:

— *Silâho... hey, é é é é! Silâho hé é é é é!*

And the echo always answered. *Ahoy, ahoy...*

The two little girls who had strayed from the road to escape the sight of Nâni showed themselves to the two older girls again.

— *But it's you that Nâni is calling!* Said Bakelâmio.

— *Who is it?* Asked Zubâbela.

— *It's Silâho and Nkâri!*

[18] —bvûter = Draw with a landing net

[19] —Yâba = Scoop fishing

— *By the God of my father,* said Zubâbela, *you feel bad, don't you? You're called and you don't answer, but go and find Nâni who is shouting up there.*

They didn't move. Zubâbela shouted in turn to call her friend:

— *Nâni hé hé hé! Ah! Nâni hé hé hé!*

And the echo answered very quickly, as the sound came from the bottom of a V. It had the thick clumps of plants foliage on either side of the river as a close ceiling.

Zubâbela uttered a prolonged *hou ou ou bi hi hi.*

Nâni is a very nimble girl, with a lively temperament. Her limbs seemed to encumber her, and yet she walked fast. She had just left in search of the Silâho, but it was likely that she was already far away.

The *hou... bi* had reached her at the rendezvous point, a short distance behind the place where they would reprimand the two little girls.

So Nâni had understood that she was being called and that the Silâho had probably introduced themselves. She was surprised at the speed with which the girls had returned to the village. Thinking of Nkâri, who is so stubborn and doesn't usually abandon the idea in her head, she was convinced that the two girls had taken a different path and had gone fishing for *yâba*.

So she answered the call with a very long *hou...bi*.

The two older girls cried out in surprise because Nâni had her way of answering the *hou... bi*. She stretched her vocal cords, which became like those of a fetish guitar, then pushed her *hou... bi* with her whole chest and her head raised.

Nâni took her legs to her neck toward the River Hôzi, to the fishing place, and a few minutes later she appeared before her companions. She was panting, and a few drops of sweat were beading on the tip of her nose. She never sweated again and even gave the reason: because she was born in the dry season. Those who sweat a lot were born in the rainy season. This is no secret.

Nâni asked:

— *So you heard me and didn't want to answer me* (she gave two lashes on the heads so as not to waste her time). *This is the reward for my breathlessness and sweat! Give me your dishes and go and cut wood to dam the river. You've come to look for work, haven't you? Go ahead and don't fight back!*

The two little girls took the machetes and obeyed without protesting about the slaps they received, because they knew the final reward: their share after fishing.

While the older girls brought back big logs to obstruct the river, the Silâho brought back twigs and clay to obstruct more effectively.

Everything was obstructed at the front and at the back. To prevent the water coming from upstream from breaking through the dam, they practised a clever irrigation system to allow the water to continue its course while deflecting it.

To do this, they ran the water between the two dams by throwing it backwards with the dishes help that they alternately immersed in the artificial pond. Meanwhile, the Silâho watched over the dams, plugging from time to time with mud, the places through which the water was seeping.

When the water receded, fish were seen trapped in the pond and they rushed to cut them out with their machetes, or, catching them in the bowl, they were thrown to the ground, and the Silâho rushed in. The operation is then quick and precise.

They hurry because the irrigated water has only one small exit, and as it accumulates in front of the dam, it tends to break it down. This requires a certain celerity that requires a vigilant eye. As this fishing is only carried out in places where the water is stagnant, it's a titanic task, especially for women.

Sometimes the place is full of fish, then it's a real miracle fishing.

You have to have a keen eye, it's true, and you have to know how to do it. You work in turbulent waters, where multicoloured dead leaves are floating and the water is moving. You have to know how to distinguish fish from black, grey or yellow leaves.

When the contents of the bowl are thrown onto the shore and a fish is caught in it, it may struggle so much that it slips into the water and goes away forever. This is the occasion for insults and mockery.

— *Ah, to eat them is good! But when you have*

to make an effort, it's bitter. Seeing a mbônghi dish is nice, but you have to know how to make it!

And many other lines, sometimes even more boring. It's therefore necessary that the yâbeuse or the tôteuse meet certain conditions for this fishing.

The two teams were busy watching each other. The fish collected by the team standing on the bank formed a tempting pile. The water had dried up, and the yâbeuse team was turning over the dead wood, opening notches on the riverbank, and pulling out wriggling fish. They were big catfish, eels and tilapia and other fish whose names were unknown.

The water upstream was still eroding the dam, and the mud kept falling. At one point, a furious swell caused a corner of the dam to collapse, despite the bold manoeuvre of the two little girls.

Nâni gave a cry of despair and jumped onto the bank; the other two older girls rushed in so suddenly that Zubâbela's dish fell and was swept away by the water. Zubâbela tried to catch it, but the waters carrying the trunks, twigs and the mudflow carried her away, so that she too fell and rolled into the avalanche.

Nkâri cried out in despair and the company began to cry and run downstream to try to catch her too.

Zubâ had rolled twice and raised her head above the water when she clung by a lucky chance, to a mangrove root that was plunging into the water.

Nâni rushed over and held out her hand; Bakelâmio got naked and immediately threw herself into the water without any hesitation. She was from Maniânga, a country of fishermen. And she could swim.

They saved their comrade from embarrassment, while Silâho and Nkâri cried their eyes out.

Zubâbela, without thinking about the accident she had just escaped, cried even harder, because she wondered where she could find another dish to replace that of Silâho's mother.

Silâho's mother is a grumbler. She has a bad tongue and often casts spells on her neighbours. She considers herself the poorest in the village and Silâho, her only daughter, she declares untouchable.

It's said that one day she got angry with a

neighbour when she went to help her niece who had just given birth. She dragged her angry buttocks across the floor. Three days later, the neighbour's daughter died without disease and the corn and peanut field dried up. The village chief decided to expel her, after a round table of families, and she was forced to pay a heavy fine.

Nkâri and Silâho finally calmed down, and by the river they discovered the bowl and brought it back. Everything was back in order.

They immediately proceeded to divide the fish and each of them got their share, considering the operations carried out by the yâbeuse and the tôteuse. This was already a lot, and each received the share they deserved. Zubâbela was given three big catfish for the mission accident, and no one expressed any displeasure. It was so normal.

They returned to the village. And while the older girls went to cook for themselves, Silâho and Nkâri presented the *ntôta*[20] to their mothers.

Going to ask Mâ Kônda for tobacco, her friend Mâ Ûmba saw the little Nkâri quivering as she opened the small *fûnda*[21] to their mothers.

[20] — Ntôta = Fruits of labour.

[21] —Fûnda = little bundle.

She exclaimed:

— *He yâye muâna'u* / Ah! this child. *Ni mayela mô* / You aren't stupid. *Where did you go fishing?*

— *At the River Hôzi, near the m'sâmpa of Tâ Bitêmo.*

— *Oh yes! Near the pond, under the foot of the big mangrove tree, right?*

— *Yes, that's right. Oh, thank God!*

— *Why thank God?*

— *Without this mangrove, we might have a death in the village, in the Tâ Ntângu District.*

— *Who is it?*

— *Zubâbela surprised by the avalanche of the broken dam.*

— *Hum, hum! This one lives only from fishing. Maybe she has a wizard's secret. She must have some initiation with the water spirits. This girl isn't to be followed at all, she might initiate you into dark fraternities, likely to ask you for souls. Then you will become a witch. You will be asked for your father, your mother one of your brothers and sisters spirits.*

— *Ha! Ha!* Said Nkâri's mother, in a dry, sour tone, but in a low voice. *The day you do something stupid like that, you will give your arm. You shall not speak to your mother's name. You shall not speak the name of your father, nor that of your brothers or sisters; you shall only dare to condemn yourself to heaven in pain. If you do this out of ignorance or knowingly, you will be cursed for life.*

The little girl began to whimper. What a nasty surprise. On the way home, the two girlfriends were telling each other many things and congratulating each other on the day's *ntôta*!

Silâho said:

— *I, at home, we had nothing to eat this evening, fortunately I managed like a big girl and my parents will be able to eat.*

And Nkâri,

— *Thanks to me, today my father will reappear at the mbônghi to taste a more substantial dish.*

— *You know, we have to get, by like this. Some women rely on their husbands, and when they have nothing, they and their children starve. For a woman, this is stupid.*

— *Indeed! To be a woman and especially a mother and not know how to garden, or ignore wild vegetables to cheat the belly is sheer madness. The belly is just a fool. Once it's full, it's satisfied. We must appease it by all means. It's so easy.*

It all made sense earlier, but now it's all falling apart. Nkâri is subject to criticism.

With the index finger of her left finger, Mâ Kônda spreads and searches the fish while commenting:

— *Just for these small spoils, you will pronounce my name to the sorcerer.*

She gave a hiccup-like gasp and continued on.

— *You, Nkâri, it's true, your name rhymes with what we didn't think of you. We thought we were saying the opposite and throwing smoke in the eyes of others... alas, you're really a bankrupt business!*

Mâ Lukûzi, who was watching the *ntôta* with attention, noticed the big fish, and soon attracted the attention of her cousin, Nkâri's mother.

— *Eh, kâni, ba sidi bâka kuâu*/Eh! No! They had a good catch!

Then she interrupted the gossipy woman:

— *Ah! Kâtuka, ni wo kuâ wekâ zonzêla mpîmpa yâ m'kâka! Are you the only subject of conversation, whose soul we will sell to the wizard?*

Mâ Kônda pushed the fûnda close to her cousin and said:

— *Go ahead, prepare some. What are you waiting for?*

Meanwhile, at Silâho's house, everything was going well. Her mother congratulated her daughter on her entrepreneurial spirit which would let her, to earn a living. She was a clever girl.

— *Even if I were to die, she could feed herself. No! My daughter will be happy. During the caterpillar season, she goes out early in the morning on an empty stomach. She runs to the river for her ablutions and goes straight to the caterpillar collection. She always comes back with something and often helps out the whole house. The same goes for winged termites, big crickets and mushrooms, and she has the courage to work in the fields.*

Silâho was a hard-working woman with a commendable courage. However, her mother overdid it and made her offspring legendary.

At Zubâbela's house, her cousin's cousin had come with her husband to give two lady cans of palm wine. In honour of a nephew who died six months ago. For reasons of force majeure, these cousins didn't come to pay their respects.

The Congolese have also known for a very long time that: *better late than never.*

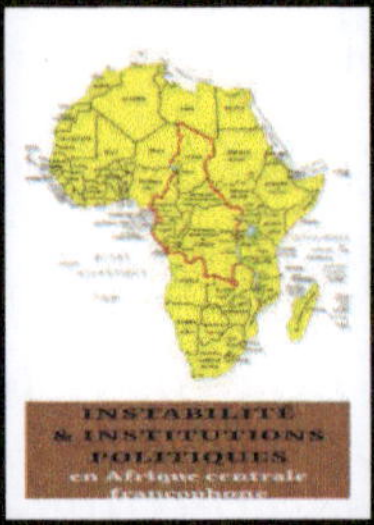

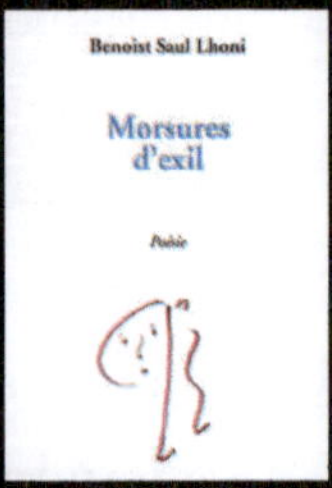

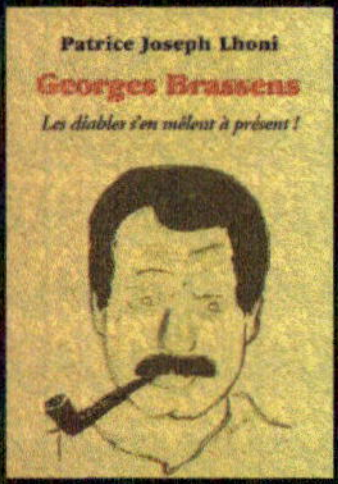

BoD Editions

www. bod.fr/librairie/